Disco Food Court

Jim Kreuch

For Tony and Jeannie

And Bob and Carol

1) The Party

The aromas of lilacs, azaleas and roses in full bloom, with a hint of freshly cut grass, filled the air. It was a warm night in early May, the full moon bigger than life, floating just above the horizon. A cloud hovered above the bright orb as if a curtain had just risen in anticipation of a performance. Birds circled, understudies awaiting their chance. It was quiet except for the chirping of crickets and the occasional distant whoosh of automobile tires on pavement. I sat atop the cinder-block wall licking my paws, my tail curled up behind me, ready for a show. Before long I had determined that the man in the moon didn't have anything to offer that I had not seen before. A critic in the form of a rudely barking dog agreed with me. The lights in the ground floor windows of a few of the houses blinked off as the early risers went upstairs to their bedrooms. On my right was the back yard of a house, the first of nine standing side by side. On my left an alleyway stretched the length of the block. Another wall stood on the other side of the alley, beyond which were another nine houses facing the opposite way. The dwellings were all pretty much the same; red brick, pitched roofs, clean and well maintained though aging, somewhat larger than an average house. I stood up and silently began to make my way along the top of the wall back toward my house at the other end of the block. There were no interesting smells emanating from any of the trash cans, humans having come to noisily empty them into the big truck that morning. I've heard that there are no alleys in the newer part of town where the rows of back yards are divided only by a wall. They only put out the trash once a week, in the front of the house by the street. The poor cats over there have only a few hours for scavenging and then nothing for another week. Sure makes you appreciate what you've got, hearing about those less fortunate.

Half way down the block I stopped and let out a meow. This is the house where my sister lives. Of the eight of us in the litter only two found homes in this neighborhood. Humans insist on splitting us up as soon as possible, since ownership of any more than three cats at a time is for some reason considered an indication of mental instability. We haven't seen the others since and couldn't say how many, if any, are still at the old house. After a few meows could be heard from within the house the screen door opened and out came a pretty cat, its pale fur silvery in the moonlight. She bounded across the neatly trimmed grass and leaped gracefully onto the wall, seemingly all in one motion.

"Good evening, your highness." We're not actually royalty, you see, it's just that her name is *Princess.* And once your human gives you a name, that's it, you're stuck with it for all nine of your lives. Don't ask me why.

"Good evening, Clarence," she replied.

"Any word on your fate?" I asked, referring to the fact that the elderly woman with whom Princess resided would soon be giving up her house. The retirement home in the faraway town to where she was moving did not allow pets. Princess was determined to find a new home in the neighborhood.

"Not a clue. Rest assured, though, if she tries to send me away I'll run off and become an alley cat. *I will!* Say, what's that racket?" She stood on the wall, her tail swaying slowly back and forth. Princess was referring to a sound coming from the far end of the block. It was rising and falling like waves crashing against a shore, but sharper and more varied.

"The Bennetts are having a party," I replied, referring to the humans who inhabit the house where I happen to live. It was a special occasion, the family not usually inclined to such activity on a school night.

"Oh, fun! Want to watch?" Without waiting for an answer she trotted off down the wall and I followed. We hopped down into the alley to cross to the other side. There we encountered two cats briskly walking by. They were young cats who lived in the alley, kittens really, named Roscoe and Muffin. The pair simultaneously turned to approach us as if joined by an invisible harness.

"Hello Princess. Clarence," said Roscoe.

"We're going to go play in the traffic," added Muffin. "Care to join us?"

"No thanks," I replied. "You youngsters go right ahead. We're going to watch the goings-on at the Bennetts." Don't get me wrong, I love playing in the traffic. It's just that I'm down to only five lives, having been shot once and run over by two cars and a delivery truck. I'm sure those two kittens still have eight or nine lives apiece left. As the kitties ran off toward the street Princess and I jumped over the wall and into the back yard of the Bennett house.

7

Ben Bennett made a small fortune when he sold the mid-western farm that was left to him when his father passed away. He had good intentions of keeping it in the family but, having little inclination for the agricultural life, couldn't resist accepting a generous offer from an investor. It seems that the purchaser was confident that the acreage would soon be in demand for shopping centers and housing developments. His brother-in-law in the planning department had divulged some inside information as to the path of a new beltway that would soon encircle the nearby city. The Bennett land just happened to be situated adjacent to a proposed exit ramp. So Ben cashed in and moved his family to our town. He decided to purchase an automobile dealership. For Ben Bennett, you see, was a natural born salesman. He lived to sell. Closing a deal was like oxygen to Ben. He shook hands vigorously while smiling easily and broadly, distracting his targets from the assassin's look in his eyes. Starting out with a lemonade stand when he was five, he graduated to band candy then lied about his age to get a job selling magazine subscriptions door-to-door at the age of fourteen. Eventually he graduated to retailing farm equipment, but soon grew bored with it. Selling people what they *needed* just wasn't challenging enough for him. Selling people what they *wanted*, and maybe a little bit more, that was more like it.

That's a perfectly good car there, sir, but I'm sure a man with your impeccable taste would be happier with this fine automobile over here. V-8 engine, leather seats, automatic transmission...

How do I know all of this, you might ask. It's simple. Over the years I've eavesdropped on numerous conversations between the various members of the Bennett family. When they're talking, humans don't seem to be the least bit concerned that cats are in the room. It's as though they think we don't know what they're talking about.

"There's Gramps," said Princess. We sat down on the grass next to a big old gray cat who was looking into the den where the party was in full swing. With the sliding-glass door wide open and only the screen door between us and the action, we could hear everything. "So Clarence, what's the occasion?"

"It's a birthday party for the daughter, Mary Ann. It's her seventeenth. That's her over there with her parents." Mary Ann was always a tad overweight, had braces on her teeth, and wore the most unflattering plastic-frame eyeglasses. Inclined to shyness, she had been quite the bookworm early in her high school career. Then midway through junior year she surprised everyone by taking up swimming to shed some weight, losing the braces, and switching to contact lenses. Suddenly she was popular enough to make a serious run at homecoming queen, finishing third, while still managing to keep her grades respectable.

"She seems awfully sweet," sighed Princess. "Look at how pretty she looks in her blue sun dress. I wish she would adopt me."

Just then Mary Ann's five-year-old brother Joey entered the room. He approached his sister and handed her a small box crudely wrapped in tissue paper. A bow that had surely decorated at least one previous gift was affixed by a generous helping of cellophane tape. A scrap of notebook paper was included in lieu of a birthday card, *Mary Ann* written thereon in crayon. The second *N* was somewhat smaller than the preceding characters due to the author's initial optimism as to the amount of room available on the tiny sheet. Mary Ann peeled away the wrapping, opened the box and pulled out a gold chain on which was attached a red gemstone.

"Wow, is that a real ruby?"

"I dunno," said the child.

"Well whatever it is, I love it." By her manner it was obvious that she thought the ruby to be a cheap trinket and not the real thing. "Here, help me put it on," she said, holding the two ends of the necklace behind her head, the stone resting against her neck. She got down on one knee so Joey could reach and then held her hair up out of the way. The boy managed to fasten the clasp with some difficulty. The chain being sufficiently long, the stone hung well below the neckline of Mary Ann's dress and had dropped down behind the fabric unnoticed by her. As a result, none of the other humans saw the stone. Gramps had crept up to the sliding-glass doors and was staring in the direction of the birthday girl.

"What's up, Gramps?" I asked as Princess and I sidled up to the glass.

"That is quite a stone there on that necklace."

"Do you think it's a real ruby?" asked Princess.

"Hard to tell without a closer look, but I would wager that it's a fake. I mean, a real ruby that size would be worth a small fortune. Humans wouldn't leave something like that lying around where a five-year-old can get to it. Or would they?"

Just then the screen door slid open and a teenage couple, hand in hand, stepped outside and hurried to a dark corner of the yard, the girl giggling all the way. Gramps darted through the opening and Princess and I followed before anyone realized the screen had been left open. Gramps and Princess slipped behind the sofa as I distracted the humans by walking right through the crowded room and letting out a loud meow. A girl knelt down and said, "Awww, look at the pretty kitty." I let her pet me long enough to allow my cohorts to reach the other end of the sofa and then sauntered over to meet them. The rendezvous took place beneath an end table where we were hidden from view but could peek out to see what was going on.

A boy of about the same age as Joey wandered through the crowd, desperately seeking the company of someone his own size. Spotting Joey he approached and said, "watchya doin'?"

"Nuthin," was the reply. "I gave my sister the necklace."

"What necklace?"

"The one I found in the box."

"What box?"

"Gee dummy, can't you remember anything? The box with the post cards and junk. My dad said I could have whatever I want out of it."

"Oh."

We watched as Mary Ann sat down to open presents, her mother dutifully taking notes in order to insure that the proper thank you cards would be sent. Born Betty Kowalski, Mrs. Bennett was eighteen months older than her husband. They had become acquainted when they were children, as Betty was best friends with Ben's older sister. Betty was well liked by practically everyone. She had a pleasing demeanor and an easy smile that made people feel at ease. More than once perfect strangers had confided in her, revealing some deep dark secrets in the process. She was not unattractive, but not of sufficient beauty to incite jealousy in the cheerleaders and other popular girls. Betty's one outstanding feature was her gorgeous head of red hair which she wore shoulder-length and wavy. Ben had developed a crush on her in high school, but for a very long time she paid him no mind. He was nothing if not determined, though. Eventually she, a senior, condescended to be his date for the junior prom. The rest, as they say, is history. Betty did well to marry a man with earning potential, as she had a habit of excelling in all the subjects that offered much intellectually but little financially. After earning a bachelor's degree in philosophy and a master's in English literature she was well qualified for teaching, food service, and little else that offered a steady paycheck. So she stayed home with the kids and wrote short stories, so far unpublished by any of the numerous literary magazines to which she mailed them on a regular basis. She finally decided to give up on this particular form of expression and began to write a play about a love triangle involving a paralegal, a paramedic, and a paranoid. At the time of our story she was on page three.

In addition to the necklace, Mary Ann netted two sweaters, one box of imported chocolates, three compact discs, five romance novels, and four cards that each contained a twenty-dollar bill. Not bad. Once the gift wrapping had been disposed of and the gifts set neatly aside on a shelf over by the fireplace, Mary Ann and her parents stepped into the dining room where awaiting them was a white sheet cake the size of a traffic sign with the words *Happy Seventeenth Mary Ann* written in blue frosting. If you haven't guessed by now, blue is Mary Ann's favorite color. As the birthday girl cut the cake and placed the scrumptious cubes on little paper plates, her mom and dad added little plastic forks and distributed the treats to the guests.

"There's punch in the kitchen," said Mrs. Bennett to one guest after another, "and coffee too." Mary Ann's two best friends, a blonde girl and a brunette, had been tabbed for beverage duty. Mary Ann's other brother Max, two years her junior, stood within earshot of our end table devouring two pieces of cake.

"They haven't put you to work?" came a woman's voice coming from somewhere above us.

"Don't worry, Aunt Martha. I'll be the one stuck with cleaning up this mess later."

Max and his sister had gradually exchanged places in the high school social and academic pecking order. As Mary Ann's star was rising his was headed due south. The boy had been the best striker on his middle-school soccer team, nearly able to score goals at will. At an overall higher level of play in high school he was reduced from outstanding to merely above average. His playing time reduced, he had lately taken to spending more and more time with video games while neglecting his exercise and slacking off at practices. As a result, the pounds his sister lost stayed in the family in the form of a meatier, beefier Max. He was also getting more and more bored with school. While his sister could sit through a lecture and soak up information like a sponge, he was inclined to learning by doing. Max had an aptitude for things mechanical. Give him a broken washing machine or a car that wouldn't start and he would figure it out, more often than not without the aid of a manual. While this talent was not unappreciated in his family, it would never carry the status of academic achievement.

The guests had abandoned their places in the den, swarming around the cake and liquid refreshments in the kitchen. One by one they returned like school children reclaiming their desks after recess. A young man of perhaps nineteen years and average height, muscular enough for outdoor work, entered the room. His brown hair was of a length that suggested a haircut might have been had some days ago but could just as well be done within the coming week. He wore white denim trousers, an apron, and a bright orange shirt. No one thought him oddly dressed as everyone in the room knew him to be Mary Ann's boyfriend Pete, gainfully employed as the assistant manager of an ice cream parlor. Not wishing to miss any more of the festivities than absolutely necessary, he had come directly from work without changing from his uniform into something more appropriate. The stains on his white apron revealed the day's most popular flavor to be chocolate, with orange sherbet a close second.

"There you are!" exclaimed Mary Ann as she waded through the crowd. "You can take off the apron now." The boyfriend being a foot taller, she stood on her tiptoes in order to throw her arms around his neck. She puckered up and closed her eyes but waited in vain for a kiss. Pete stared into space and mumbled to no one in particular, "I left it in the car." Mary Ann waited three seconds longer then opened her eyes.

"Left what, sweetie?" she asked as she reached around to untie his apron.

"I left your present in the car," he murmured, blushing.

"So go get it!" she laughed. "But first give me a kiss." She puckered up again and settled for a quick one, the boyfriend suddenly aware that everyone in the room was looking in the couple's direction. He hurried out of the room, turning back just long enough to say, "Be right back." Returning shortly he carried a large paper sack of the variety one must specifically request at the grocery store, plastic bags being the default container nowadays.

"Sorry, I didn't have time to wrap it. Or buy a card."

"That's okay," said Mary Ann as she swapped a cup of punch and a piece of cake for the present, "you've been working a lot of hours." She set the sack on the kitchen counter, reached in, and pulled out an exquisitely detailed wood carving of a bear. "It's beautiful," she said, gently setting the statue down. "Where did you get it?"

"You know the old trading post up on fifty-eight?" He paused to lick some frosting off of his upper lip. Pete was referring to Highway 58, two lanes of asphalt that had been the main westbound road out of town until a wider highway was installed running parallel a half mile to the south. "The place with all the weird stuff? I stopped there for gas a couple of weeks ago. They have all these really great wood carvings. When you ask the owner where he gets them he just smiles and says, "trade secret."

Once Mary Ann had sufficiently admired the gift and expressed her gratitude she made the rounds, graciously exchanging pleasantries with as many people as possible.

"Oh, I so want her to adopt me," sighed Princess.

"Yes, so you've said," I replied.

"That cake sure looks good," said Princess with a particular mischief in her voice that only cats can produce. By then the humans were gathering around Mr. Bennett at the far end of the room. It seemed a speech of some sort was forthcoming. Most took their refreshments with them, but a few had left behind half-eaten pieces of cake. Looking up, I spotted a plate just protruding from the top of the end table under which we were hiding.

"I've got this," I said. Standing on my hind legs I quickly reached up and knocked it onto the floor. Someone had taken a piece, a big one from the corner of the cake, and for whatever reason abandoned the mouth-watering item after taking but a single bite.

"Pay dirt!" said Gramps.

"Nice work, brother," added Princess. I admit to feeling rather pleased with myself at that juncture. The cake, of course, had landed frosting side down on the carpet. Not that it mattered. Gramps swatted away the little paper plate and plastic fork and the three of us went to town on that cake. We had scarfed it down and sucked all of the frosting out of the rug fibers before Mr. Bennett could clear his throat.

"Friends, family, neighbors," said Ben. The man had what could be described as a *booming* voice, and he was apparently determined to use it to full effect this evening. The words reached every pair of ears in the house. In order to be seen by all, he was standing on the second rung of a small stepladder. "First, I would like to thank you all for being here to celebrate my daughter Mary Ann's seventeenth birthday. Mary Ann, here's to many more!" With this he raised his plastic glass of punch, causing him to momentarily lose his balance and sway back and forth. The applause from the crowd was interspersed with the odd *ooh* or *aah* in concern for the speaker's safety. He managed to recover without spilling a drop and continued his speech without missing a beat.

At this point I stepped out from under the end table to take a survey of the room. Every human's attention was now fixed on Ben, who had erected his makeshift podium at the far end of the dining room. I motioned my comrades to venture forth. There were several more partially eaten pieces of cake to be had on the coffee tables. Oh, how I love a party! As we grazed Ben Bennett spoke of how it seemed like yesterday that they brought his baby girl home from the hospital, recollected the day the training wheels came off her bike, and heaped praise on her for her academic achievements.

"And now, if Mary Ann will pardon me, I would like to take this opportunity to make an announcement." He stepped down just long enough to rid himself of the punch glass then returned to the ladder, this time standing on the very top with his head just inches from the ceiling. "I hereby declare that I am a candidate for the office of mayor of our fair city." He thrust out his arms like a conductor at the crescendo. This was followed by the usual promises of honesty, integrity and better ways of *getting things done*, the sort of things politicians say on occasions such as this. After a warm round of applause the guests began to say their goodbyes and file out through the front door. It was, after all, a school night.

Some of the guests having taken their refreshments on the patio, Max slid open the screen door and began to pick up the paper plates and plastic cups. Gramps and Princess took this opportunity to slip outside unobserved. With no need for stealth in my own home, I could be more casual in following them. Shortly thereafter the young man stepped back inside and shut the screen door, saying to no one in particular, "okay, the patio's cleaned up and the cat's out."

"Well, I'm going home to take a nap," said Gramps, "but I have something I've been wanting to discuss with you two. What do you say you come over tomorrow afternoon at two? My human will be out all the afternoon, so we'll have the place to ourselves."

2) The Mannequin

After roaming around for the better part of the night, Princess and I parted and returned to our respective homes. I curled up on the front porch and took a nap, not wanting to be stuck inside when it was time to visit Gramps. I was about to doze off just as the morning sun was feeding the leaves on the uppermost tree branches while those below waited their turn. Suddenly the front door abruptly swung open and Max charged across the threshold, over the lawn, and down the street just in time to catch the school bus. I went to sleep. I awoke when the grandfather clock in the front room struck two. A sunny, warm May day was perfect for sleeping, but I had business to attend to. I got up to stretch.

"Boo!"

I jumped up and did a one-eighty in mid-air, landing (of course) on my feet. I found myself face to face with Princess who had done a masterful job of sneaking up on me.

"Good one," I said, for although she had scared the daylights out of me, a cat always appreciates and acknowledges a good *sneak job* and would never take it personally. You see, cats are just as good at sneaking up on each other as we are at sneaking up on anything else. It's one of our favorite sports. After exchanging pleasantries we padded across the street and over to Gramps' house, arriving a few minutes past the hour. We had made a slight detour in order to chase a butterfly across a yard. There was no need to apologize for our tardiness, since cats are generally not expected to conform to any degree of punctuality.

We entered the back yard by squeezing through an opening between a weathered wooden gate and the gate post. Then we circled around to the back porch and the door which the human habitually left cracked open in the summer for ventilation. Gramps' house is older and larger than the others in the neighborhood. He tells me that it originally stood all by itself outside of town, having been built as the country summer home of a wealthy family whose patriarch had made his fortune in silver mining. The house, complete with stables for the horses the family rode, overlooked several wooded acres and a picturesque fishing pond. The stables are long gone, leaving only the house on a quarter-acre lot, now surrounded by the subdivision's newer homes. The house stands out not only because it's three stories tall, but because of the several prominent chimneys and gables. A city street now separates the house and the pond, which is the centerpiece of a neighborhood park.

In response to our meows, Gramps nudged open the screen door until the opening was just wide enough for a cat.

"Come on in."

Not waiting for a second invitation, I tiptoed through the opening, Princess following close behind.

"It's nice and cool in here," I said, curling up on the sofa.

"Yes," added Princess. "Very pleasant."

"My human always leaves the cooler running on 'low' when he steps out for a while."

"That's awfully nice of him," she said.

"Or forgetful," I added.

"Neither," said Gramps. "You see, he's just following instructions."

"Instructions?" said Princess and I simultaneously, looking at each other.

"That's right, instructions."

"Instructions from... whom?" I ventured.

"Well, from me, of course," said the old gray cat, looking rather smug. "Let me explain..."

Princess hopped onto the sofa and curled up beside me as if expecting a lengthy speech. Gramps climbed onto the coffee table and sat down facing us, pausing as if to consider his words carefully.

"My friends," he began, "I'm afraid I may be the only one left, at least in our town, who is well versed in the art of *focused purring*."

"*Focused* purring?" Princess' head tilted to one side as she gave him a curious look. "What's that?"

"Focused purring is a human behavior modification technique. When you've mastered the art you can transmit instructions to your human and influence their decision making."

"That's for real?" I said, remembering that I'd heard of this sort of thing before. "I thought that stuff was just superstition."

"It does sounds a bit far-fetched," said Princess.

"Oh, not at all," replied Gramps patiently. "It's a tried and true method, practiced by cats for centuries. And it's useful not just for mundane things like getting humans to upgrade the cat food. Cats have used it to inspire a number of men and women throughout history to greatness. Sir Winston Churchill, Florence Nightingale, Teddy Roosevelt, Joe Namath. All cat people. "

"You don't say?"

"I do say. And cats have purred some very famous authors into creating some outstanding literature. Mark Twain, T.S. Eliot, the Brontë sisters. And Ernest Hemingway, he shared his property in Cuba with dozens of cats."

"You're telling us that cats made these people do things they wouldn't have otherwise done?" She looked skeptical.

"Absolutely. Take Mr. Namath, for example. Any sports fan will tell you that coaches frown on players giving quotes to the press that could end up on the opposing team's bulletin board. Joe knew better than to mouth off with that "guaranteed win" line. There's no doubt in my mind that it was Poppet's idea."

"So if this focused purring is such a great thing, why aren't all the cats doing it?" I asked.

"Sadly it's fallen into disuse in modern times. Not only is there an appalling lack of interest shown by the younger generation of cats, but humans have changed. Back in the day, they were so much more manageable. A fellow would spend his evenings by the fire with a good book, cat on his lap or curled up by the fire. Plenty of time to get a good purr going. Nowadays they're such restless, distracted creatures. If they're not flipping through the TV channels with the remote control, they're getting up to answer the phone or hopping in the car to run over to the store for something or other. And don't get me started on all the crazy drivers out there! I used to wander around town all the time, but it's just not safe crossing so many of the streets anymore. I don't take any chances now, you know, being down to my last two lives before I'm off to Kitty Heaven. It wasn't always like this, you know... but I digress. So would you like to learn it?"

"Can I use it to convince Mary Ann to adopt me?" asked Princess, standing up on the sofa.

"Yes, of course."

"Then I'd love to."

"Me too," I chimed in.

"Good, good, I'm glad there are at least a couple of younger cats that are willing to learn. These days the kitties only care about feeding their faces, playing in the traffic, and snorting catnip. Anyway," he continued, "focused purring, as the name implies, is a way of capturing the energy released by our purring and focusing it so as to influence the thoughts of others, specifically humans. So if you'll follow me into the basement, we'll begin our lesson." He eased himself off of the coffee table and onto the floor, then led us through the kitchen and turned into a narrow stairwell.

"Mouse!" exclaimed Princess.

"Oh boy," I replied. We reversed course and pursued the little varmint across the kitchen. Princess being faster, she almost got him as he slipped through a hole behind the waste basket under the sink. Gramps peered out from the stairwell.

"If you two would kindly get your minds off of food for a moment, we'll begin..."

The two small windows just below the basement's ceiling provided more than enough light for us to see everything in the room. And an odd sight it was. Among the usual garden tools, dust-covered exercise equipment, and cardboard boxes one expects to find in a basement, stood half a dozen mannequins. Or, I should say, stood five mannequins, one being seated on an old kitchen chair.

"Are those people?" whispered Princess, her eyes wide.

"No, silly," replied Gramps, "they're just leftover mannequins from the store."

"What store?"

"The old clothing store downtown, the one my human used to own. It was the finest store in town. Had a first class jewelry counter too. Did quite well for himself, that is until business dropped off after the shopping mall opened. By then, though, he had saved up enough to be set for life, so he shut down the store and retired."

"What does he do now?" I ventured.

"Well... he spends a lot of time on the golf course. That's where he is today, so I don't expect him back for hours. Now, for lesson number one. First you must be sure that your human, the human must be a cat person, not a dog person but a cat person..."

"Understood."

"Anyway, make sure that your human is in a sitting position as we see here." Gramps stood before the seated mannequin. "Truly effective focused purring can only be achieved when the human is in a sitting position."

"Why is that?" asked Princess. "And how do you get them to sit down?"

"Good questions. I'll answer the first one first. You see, purring releases a form of energy for lack of a better word. And this energy, like heat, rises. When you're sitting in the lap, energy reaches the human's brain with a minimum of dissipation and therefore maximum effectiveness. And this brings us to your second question, how to get them to sit. You can try rubbing against their legs while purring. This can be effective in getting a human to sit down, provided they're not being distracted by an electronic device of some sort at the time. If they've got a smart phone or a remote control in their hands, forget it. You'll never get their attention. Frankly, you'll probably just have to wait for them to settle down. This was so much easier in the old days!"

"Can't you just wait for them to go to bed?" I asked.

"Another good question. Unfortunately when they're lying down it doesn't work unless you sit right on top of their heads. For some reason this upsets them. So Princess, hop up onto the lap of the mannequin and make yourself comfortable. I know it's not the same as a live one, but do the best you can. Okay, now close your eyes and relax." The old cat began to whisper, "A can of sardines...little white mice...a lovely ball of yarn..." It wasn't long before she was purring contentedly. "Now pretend you're on Mary Ann's lap. Focus on her and think about what it is you want her to do."

"Adopt me... adopt me... adopt me..."

"Very good," said Gramps. "Clarence, you try it now."

I climbed onto the mannequin, curled up and closed my eyes and tried to think happy thoughts. It was no use. I felt perfectly silly sitting there on a dummy like I was trying to send it my thoughts.

"It's not happening," I said. "I feel silly."

"Nonsense," replied Gramps sharply. "You've just got to play a little make-believe. That's not a mannequin, it's Mary Ann. Or Ben or Betty or whoever works for you."

"Okay, I'll try." I thought of last Friday evening when the Bennetts had grilled salmon for dinner and hadn't given me any despite my best efforts to look hungry and pathetic. I pretended the mannequin was Betty Bennett and imagined her wrapping up the leftovers, except that this time she stopped and tossed me a nice chunk of the savory fish...

"There you go, that's it," said Gramps triumphantly. "Now when you do it for real, you'll be aware of a connection with the human's mind. That's how you'll know it's working. The link is sort of like telepathy except that it's entirely one-sided, the poor human remaining blissfully unaware of what's being done. Give it a try when you get home. Clarence, what kind of cat food do they usually give you?"

"Dry. Always the dry stuff."

"There you go. You can use this technique to have one of the humans bring home the expensive canned cat food from the store. Once you've accomplished that task, sit on Mary Ann's lap and purr, focusing on how much happier she would be with two cats instead of one.

Princess, try it on your human. Focus on letting her know that Mary Ann is good with cats. Then all you have to do is hang around at the Bennetts house looking sweet and innocent."

"Oh boy, I can't wait."

"Now let's go upstairs," said Gramps. "These mannequins give me the creeps."

Princess spotted another mouse and gave chase. This time she was successful and graciously presented our host with the little carcass.

"Thanks, dear, that's very thoughtful of you. I'll eat it later."

I went home and waited on the front porch for Mary Ann to return home from her tennis lesson. As she came up the steps I gave her my best sad-kitty eyes and let out a single pathetic meow.

"Poor Clarence. Are you all alone? Let's get you a nice dish of milk."

I was purring already. Once I had slurped down the cow juice and Mary Ann had made herself comfortable on the den sofa with one of her school books, I went to work. I curled up on her lap and focused, just like Gramps said to.

"...dry cat food bad...canned cat food good...dry cat food bad..."

I could feel a connection even though she seemed involved in her studies. I kept it up for a while, though, and my efforts were rewarded. Sure enough, she picked me up and gently set me down on the floor. Then Mary Ann walked straight into the kitchen, took the shopping

Jim Kreuch

list off of the refrigerator, grabbed the car keys and bolted out the front door. After she returned from the store her mother entered the kitchen as the younger Bennett was putting the groceries away.

"What's this, you bought canned cat food?"

Mary Ann looked surprised. "That's odd," she said thoughtfully. "I didn't mean to."

Her mother examined the grocery store receipt. "It wasn't on sale. That's okay dear, Clarence deserves a treat every once in a while."

"I suppose I should get back to my books." She returned to the den with an absent minded scratch of the head.

I had passed my focused purring test with flying colors. Now it was time to set the stage for Princess to be adopted into the Bennett household. I waited until after dinner when the family was gathered in the den watching television. All except for Mary Ann, that is. She was curled up at the end of the living room sofa, dressed comfortably in a sweatshirt and some blue jeans that had seen better days. She was again reading one of her school books. There was only one electronic device in that room and it was softly playing some sort of background music. I sat on the floor at her feet with my eyes closed for a while, listening to the music and thinking of such pleasant things as butterflies, freshly killed mice, and dogs being hauled off to the pound. Once I had started purring I hopped up onto the sofa and plopped down on her lap. She unconsciously began to stroke my head and the back of my neck, just the way I like it, still engrossed in the book which she clutched in her left hand.

"...two cats are better than one...two cats are better than one..."

Later that night I met Princess in the usual place, atop the cinder block wall behind her back yard. A brief but intense late afternoon thunderstorm had left the lawns damp and everything smelling fresh. The moon was completely obscured by clouds, making it a dark night by human standards. We cats can see just fine, though, with very little light.

"So how did it go?" she asked anxiously. "Did you get them to buy you the good stuff?"

"Worked like a charm. Ah, tasty delicious moist canned cat food for dinner! I could get used to this. How about you? How did you do?"

"Not so good. My human was on the phone with the retirement home people for half an hour and then wouldn't let go of the TV remote."

"Don't worry about it. I'm pretty sure I've got Mary Ann thinking in terms of getting a second cat. All you need to do is show up tomorrow and it will be smooth sailing."

3) The Shopping Mall

The next day being Saturday, all of the Bennetts except for Ben were at home. From my perch on the back of the living room sofa, I could see that Mary Ann was gently swaying back and forth on the porch swing, reading a magazine. A perfect opportunity. Standing by the front door, I let out a stream of really annoying meows until Joey came over and let me out. I was just about to run over to fetch Princess when my sister emerged from the row of bushes that stood in front of the porch. She had ditched her collar and was doing her best to look sad and lonely. Sure enough, before two minutes had passed Princess was purring away on Mary Ann's lap. From the look on the girl's face I could tell that it was working like a charm.

"Is that Mrs. Elliot's cat, dear? Mrs. Elliot from down the street?" Betty Bennett was standing just inside the screen door. "Where's its collar?"

"I don't know, it must have come off. I heard she's going to have to give up her cat when she moves. Can we keep it?"

"Are you sure you want to take on another pet? You'll have to feed it and clean the litter box."

"No sweat. We already have Clarence, and feeding one more won't be any more trouble at all. I'll take care of the cats, I promise."

"Well okay. As long as it's okay with your father it's okay with me."

I knew from previous observation of many such instances that the approval of the nominal head of the family was a mere formality. A *slam dunk* if you will. I have no idea where that phrase comes from, but the humans sure are fond of repeating it.

A middle-aged woman wearing a cotton dress with a flower print pattern and a broad-brimmed hat walked up the sidewalk and approached the house.

"Hi Aunt Martha. Taking your walk?"

"Yes, these days are so pleasant I just had to get out and enjoy the weather. Is your mother home?"

"She is. I'll get her." With that Mary Ann gently placed Princess on the porch swing and went inside. Martha sat down and proceeded to stroke Princess' head and back. Momentarily Betty appeared through the screen door with her daughter at her heels. The latter did an abrupt about face with the first ring of a telephone and had answered it before the second ring had expired.

"Hey sis. I was just leaving for the shopping mall. I wouldn't mind some company."

"I'd be delighted. Let's go."

As soon as it was mentioned that the two-door car would be taken, Princess and I had the same idea, that is, we would tag along. Let me explain. The *tag-along* is a daring maneuver that cats use to hitch a ride, feasible only when one or two humans are going somewhere in a two-door car. The cats hide underneath the vehicle until one or both of the doors open, then quickly jump in. There's just enough room to squeeze in behind the front seats and hide on the floor. And it's got to be quick if you value your tail!

We scampered over to the driveway and hid underneath the car. I took the driver's side, Princess the passenger side. We waited patiently, ready to spring into action. The trick is to avoid the temptation to go when you hear the door open, you see, you have to wait until the human steps into the car so as to remain unobserved. Then you have to jump in quickly and reel in your tail, before they close the door. And believe me, some of these humans slam that door rather quickly. This particular time was a challenge. The two sisters approached the car and one of them, I don't know which, opened the driver's side door. Then they stood there arguing over who would drive.

"Really, I don't mind, dear," said Martha, the older of the two by several years. "You must get so tired of always running around town. Why don't you relax and let me drive? I hardly ever get to drive." I got the feeling that Betty surrendered the car keys reluctantly due to a lack of confidence in her older sister's driving skills. So Aunt Martha opened the driver's side door and started to get in, but I had to wait until Betty turned to walk around to the other side before I could make my move. It was close, but I made it without being seen and, more importantly, with my tail intact. Princess made me proud by timing her move to perfection. We were two happy little stowaways. The car made a sudden lurch and then came to a stop just as suddenly, causing Princess and I to hunker down on the floor mats and hang on.

"Oooh, this car goes faster than mine," came a voice from the driver's side of the car.

"Are you sure you don't want me to drive?"

"No, no, I'm okay. Now where's forward on this thing?"

Once Martha had found DRIVE she became overly cautious as if to make reparations for the violence of the exit from the driveway. I managed a peek at the speedometer which was holding steady at twenty miles per hour. Her sister was fidgeting nervously in the passenger seat. My friend and I spent the duration of the crosstown drive eavesdropping, the necessity of keeping still and quiet depriving us of any other form of amusement. We learned that we were on our way to Pinewood Mall, the older of the two climate-controlled shopping centers in town. It had been hemorrhaging tenants ever since the bigger, more upscale Apple Creek Mall opened on the outskirts of town. Ben had heard that it was likely he could obtain a very reasonable rate on some space there for use as his mayoral campaign headquarters. Betty was to meet with the mall manager to pick out an appropriate store front. Martha, no doubt, would seek out a bargain or two while in the neighborhood.

I felt the car come to a halt. My companion and I exchanged glances, then turned around to face our respective car doors. This time the two women disembarked simultaneously, oblivious to the fact that an unseen hitchhiker was jumping out of each door. Princess and I made our rendezvous under the car.

"Why do they call this place Pinewood?" asked Princess. "There's not a tree in sight."

"If you think that's bad, remind me to tell you about a country called Greenland some time."

"Hey, I smell fish!" said Princess.

"Fish and chips. Yummy!" Sure enough, it was the unmistakable aroma of deep-fried cod and potatoes. We had planned to follow the Bennett women into the main entrance of the mall, but changed our minds the instant we smelled fish. A *no-brainer*, as the humans would say. We ran as fast as our paws would carry us across the warm pavement, which wasn't far. Martha had parked the car close to the building, the parking lot containing only a handful of cars.

Just as we were trying to figure out how to get inside the fish and chips shop, the door flew open. Princess and I hid behind a dumpster where we could see a man step outside and lean against the wall. He was dressed in a white shirt and breeches partially covered by a bright red apron. He casually lit up a cigarette, staring into the distance at nothing in particular.

"Look," I said, "he's left the door propped open."

We wasted no time, slipping inside quicker than you can say *pass the tartar sauce*. The tiny kitchen was unoccupied except for one teenage girl, dressed identically to the man outside. She was sitting on an overturned five-gallon plastic drum, engaged in what was undoubtedly a personal call on the telephone and paid us no mind. The lunch rush was obviously over, or more likely it had never really begun. Princess and I feasted on fries and scraps of fish we found on the floor. You wouldn't believe how much perfectly good food gets dropped on the floor in fast food joints. I eyed a mouse crouching in a dark corner behind the steam table, but the fish was so good that I couldn't be bothered. Some other time, varmint.

Having gotten this far without detection by anybody with two legs, I invited my furry companion to go exploring by boldly leaping onto the counter of the fish and chips shop and into the seating area of the food court. The fish and chips shop was just one of several fast food establishments lined up one after the other forming three sides of a sizable rectangular room. The fourth wall was non-existent, the food court opening up to the main concourse of the shopping mall. Half of the little restaurants were closed down, though, the number of potential diners having of course dropped off along with the business of the other stores. Only four of the tables in the seating area were occupied. A threesome of mechanics from the tire store across the parking lot hunched over burgers and fries while a pair of clerks from the last surviving dress store sipped coffee. At the third table sat a middle-aged man in a dark blue business suit perusing a newspaper while skillfully shoveling the contents of a plastic bowl into his mouth with a pair of chopsticks.

Princess and I crept over and made ourselves comfortable underneath the fourth table where there sat another middle-aged man, this one in a light blue business suit. The fish and chips man who had been smoking outside came in and sat down. "What's the word?" he said, stirring some coffee in a disposable cup.

"Hanging in there," was the reply. The businessman was slowly shaking his head. "We're still trying to come up with a way to get some of these empty stores rented. When shoppers have to walk past too many of them they get real uncomfortable and quit coming back. The stores that are still open are having all kinds of sales, but it doesn't seem to be doing any good. The good news is that nobody has given me notice to terminate their lease today. The bad news is, the day's not over with yet. I'm telling you, if we don't get some more traffic in this place I'm afraid it's going to be lights out."

"Where's your partner?"

"She's meeting with Betty Bennett about renting some space for her husband's campaign headquarters."

"Campaign?"

"Yeah, Ben's running for mayor. Hadn't you heard?"

"News to me."

"Anyway, don't spread this around, but we're going to let them have it real cheap. I don't want everybody asking for a break, you included."

After a long pause, the fish and chips man looked around and said, "Have you thought of maybe sprucing up the food court a little? Maybe people would come here on purpose for lunch if we made it real nice. And I dunno, perhaps they would do some shopping on the way back to the car. Just a thought."

"Yeah, maybe."

From here the conversation turned to the weather and other boring topics, so Princess and I slipped out and made our way through the mall. We darted from one hiding place to another, a planter here, a trash can there, so as not to be seen. This was easily done as precious few humans were in the place. A sign in the window of a pet store caught our attention. It said:

Pet Door: lets your dog or cat come and go as they please. No more getting up to let them in and out!

We looked at each other and without a word knew that we were thinking the same thing. After we had thoroughly explored the mall it dawned on me that the Bennett gals would be leaving soon.

"Come on," I said, "we don't want to miss our ride home. It's a long walk back." We retraced our steps through the food court and the fish and chips shop back to the parking lot, taking care to stay out of the sight of the humans. "Oh no! They're gone."

"Not to worry," said Princess with a smug look on her face. "I've been studying my lady's bus schedules when she isn't looking. We can hitch a ride easily enough."

"A tag-along on the bus? That's insane!" Of course I readily agreed to it. What can I say? Cats are crazy. Princess led the way across the parking lot to the bus stop.

"The first thing you need to know is that there's two routes that serve this bus stop. We want route ten. Don't get on the number twenty-two or we'll really have a long walk back. Got it?"

"Got it." We hid behind the trash can next to the bench at the bus stop and waited. After a little while a bus arrived. I was ready to pounce until I saw a pair of deuces, big as life on the display above the windshield of the bus. We waited until a bus displaying the number ten arrived. The thing didn't stop, but just kept right on going anyway.

"Why didn't it stop?" I asked. "How are we supposed to get on if the stupid thing doesn't even slow down?"

"Hmmm... I guess they don't have any reason to stop if they don't see anybody at the bus stop. Maybe we should sit up on the bench so the next driver sees us."

"Don't be ridiculous. They're not going to stop for a couple of cats. We're just going to have to wait until a human or two show up. You've never actually done this before, have you?"

"Well.... no." We sat there feeling a bit silly for some time. Just when I was about to suggest we start walking, another bus number ten approached and this time it wheezed to a stop. "Of course!" exclaimed Princess. "It's got to stop to let people off, too."

"Why didn't I think of that?" I mumbled half aloud. As the bus came to a halt with a wheeze and a clunk, Princess started towards the door. "Psst! There's another door in the back. They'll see us if we go in the front."

"It's no good. The lady is getting off through the front door. The back one isn't opening." Princess made a mad dash for the door, which was now starting to close. I followed as fast as I could and barely made it. I fully expected to be picked up and unceremoniously tossed back onto the sidewalk, not imagining that we could possibly reach a hiding place without being seen. To my surprise we made it to a safe haven under a seat without any human batting an eyelash. Apparently the driver was too preoccupied with his driving to notice a couple of pint sized stowaways right under his nose. And the passengers, well, remarkably none of them paid us any mind at all. Each and every one of them had their eyeballs glued to a tiny screen on one kind of hand-held electronic device or another, little things stuck in their ears with the wires hanging down. They were so engrossed in texting, surfing, playing, shopping, calculating and talking that they were completely oblivious to their surroundings.

At the next stop two humans boarded the bus, followed closely by a cat. This cat just stepped right onto the bus and strutted down the aisle making no attempt whatsoever to keep out of sight. I was impressed. I recognized him as a cat I had lately seen around the neighborhood.

"Hey Princess. What are you doing here?"

"Soldier! I thought it was you. We pulled a tag-along to the old shopping mall but missed our ride home. Have you met my brother Clarence?"

"I've seen you around," he said to me. "You're the Bennett's cat aren't you?"

"The one and only," I said, quickly adding, "so far, at least."

"My humans moved in down at the other end of the block from you a couple of weeks ago."

"So how did you get a name like *Soldier*?"

"Quite by accident I'm afraid. My human found me at the scene of a dog fight where a poor mutt who had just gotten clobbered was limping away and whining like a little puppy. The big hound that had administered the beating had left the scene, so the human assumed that I was the one who had whipped the mutt. Humans do that a lot, jumping to conclusions. Anyway, he figured I was a real tough guy so they named me Soldier. I think he adopted me with the intention of gaining protection from burglars. Imagine that, a watch cat."

As we rode we told each other stories, somewhat embellished of course, of our experiences and adventures. Like most cats I'm not terribly sociable, but I could tell that Soldier was a good guy and well worth adding to my small circle of companions.

"Our stop is coming up," he said suddenly. Then he hopped up onto one of the seats, sitting right next to a human. Seeing the astonished expressions on our faces, he said, "don't worry, they wouldn't notice if I jumped up and down while playing a banjo." Soldier then proceeded to get up on his hind legs with his paws on the back of the seat in front of him. He gazed out the window until apparently spotting a landmark that told him it was time to pull the cord. He reached over the human in order to ring the bell. Need I say that the human remained oblivious, her eyes fixed on the little screen, thumbs tapping madly at the little keyboard?

4) The Food Court

That afternoon Mary Ann marched out the front door and headed down the street to where Princess lived. Her father had signed off on the request to double the number of cats residing at the Bennett residence. I followed her, of course, and carefully (and I do mean *carefully*) hid in a rose bush. I watched and listened as she rang the doorbell.

"Oh, hello. You're the Bennett girl from down the street, aren't you?"

"Yes ma'am. I'm Mary Ann."

"Come in, dear." I knew I had to be quick. The weather having cooled off, I knew I couldn't count on being able to eavesdrop through a door left ajar. I slipped in at Mary Ann's heels and parked myself under a coffee table which I selected from a collection of fine Early American furniture. Everything in the room, from nick knacks to doilies, sat neatly in its place except for some easy listening tunes that were escaping from a vintage Philco radio. Princess, busy clawing away at her scratching post, subtly gave me a wink and a nod.

"Would you like a cup of tea?"

"Yes, please. That would be nice."

The human stepped out of the living room and into the kitchen, returning shortly carrying a silver tray on which sat a ceramic teapot adorned with a floral theme, two matching cups and saucers, and containers of milk and sugar. A somewhat awkward conversation commenced primarily concerning the change in the weather. Humans sure do like to talk about the weather.

Then Mrs. Elliot said, "So to what do I owe the pleasure of this visit?"

"Well, ma'am, I understand you will be moving away soon."

"Yes, I've been in this big old house all by myself for too long." As if on cue, Princess began to slowly rub against the lady's left leg. "Well, not entirely alone since I've got Princess here to keep me company." She picked up the cat and gently placed her in her lap. "Of course, I'll have to give her up when I move."

"So I've heard," interjected Mary Ann.

"The retirement home where I'm going to live doesn't allow pets."

"If you don't mind me asking, have you found a home for...?"

"Princess."

"Have you found a home for Princess?"

"No, not yet," she said with a touch of sadness in her voice.

"Well, the reason I dropped by, honestly, is to ask if I could have your cat. I promise I'll take good care of her. We already have one cat."

"I've seen your cat. It's very pretty." Handsome, I said to myself. I'm *handsome*. Not pretty. She sat there for a moment petting Princess and then with a sigh said, "It's okay with your parents?"

"Oh yes, Mom and Dad said it's okay."

"Well all right then. I leave next Tuesday. On that day she's all yours."

"Thank you so much," said Mary Ann earnestly. She politely remained for some time, sipping her tea and keeping the conversation on life support with miscellaneous remarks about various objects in the room. Eventually Mrs. Elliot got up and set her cup and saucer on the tray. Mary Ann took this to be her cue to leave, thanked her hostess and went over to the front door. Mrs. Elliot followed and stood in the doorway remarking about how lovely the trees were this time of year, allowing me to slip out unnoticed.

By the following Thursday Princess was settled in at the Bennett house. That afternoon Mary Ann came home from school accompanied by her friends, the blonde girl and the brunette one. I never did catch their names. Mary Ann sat down on a chair, Princess promptly taking up residence on her lap. The other two girls were sprawled across the bed so I hopped up and made myself comfortable in a nice spot in between them. The eyes of a dozen wild animals looked down upon us. Nothing to be concerned about, only Mary Ann's stuffed animal collection. Flipping through the pages of a high school yearbook, the blonde girl remarked, "We need a place to hang out after school. You know, somewhere we can meet people."

"By *people* you mean boys, right?" said the brunette with a grin.

"We could go to the ice cream shop," replied the blonde when she had finished giggling.

"No, silly," said Mary Ann, "the last time we decided to make it our hangout my boyfriend almost got fired. We need to find somewhere new."

"What about the shopping mall?" said the brunette somewhat half-heartedly.

"The old one's dead," snapped the blonde, "and the new one's too far away. Even if we could get there, they don't exactly welcome teenagers there. Who are we kidding? There's nowhere for us to go in this town."

The conversation turned to typical subjects of concern to high school seniors. In the course of an hour it covered academics, fashion, extracurricular activities, employment, motor vehicles and last but not least, romance. Then it was time for Mary Ann to help with dinner and her friends to head home.

After they had left, I said to Princess, "I've got an idea."

"An idea? About what?"

"A way to get the kids a place to hang out after school."

The next afternoon I poked my head through the pet door which by now had been installed thanks to some focused purring on my part. It was a brilliant sunny warm spring day, so I trotted across the back yard, hopped up onto the wall, and walked down to the other end of the block. Soldier was curled up on the patio enjoying the sunshine. Since we had only been acquainted for a short time, I followed formal cat etiquette by sitting on the wall until he nodded his invitation for me to enter his territory.

"What brings you to the south end of the block, Clarence?"

"I came to see you," I replied. "How would you like to take a ride over to the old shopping mall?"

"Sure, I've got nothing scheduled for today. Come to think of it, I don't have anything scheduled... ever. Are you proposing a tag-along?"

"Actually I thought we'd take the bus since Princess will be joining us."

"Excellent."

"Princess and I have become quite adept at riding the bus thanks to having observed you in action."

"Glad to be of service," said Soldier, getting up and stretching.

"If you'll follow me." I retraced my steps on the cinder block wall with Soldier on my heels. In one of the yards below Roscoe and Muffin were taking turns pouncing on an inflatable pool toy.

"Hey Clarence," said the former. "What are you up to?"

"Just going to catch the bus to the shopping mall."

"Ooooh, the bus!" squealed Muffin. "I've never ridden the bus. Can we come too?" I turned around and looked at Soldier, who nodded his approval.

"Sure, why not?" I said to the kittens. "The more the merrier." So the four of us padded along the wall one after the other to the Bennett house where we were joined by Princess. Our little clowder then proceeded to cross the street and follow the sidewalk around the corner and down the hill to the bus stop that was situated in front of the park. We waited under the bench at the bus stop, all five of us. A woman with a child in tow came and sat down. The adult human didn't seem to notice us, but the kid kept peeking under the bench and babbling something or other.

"Okay," said Soldier. "Since there's five of us we're going to need to form two teams." I was happy to defer to him as the most experienced bus rider of the group. "Princess, you're with me. Clarence will take the kittens." I was beginning to suspect that Soldier had developed a romantic interest in my dear Princess. He's a decent sort of fellow, I thought. She could do worse. "We'll go in the front door with the humans, you three in the back door, assuming it opens."

"And if it doesn't?" I asked.

"Simple. You catch the next bus if it stops, or the one after that. This time of day they run about every ten or twelve minutes, tops. Then we can meet up at the mall."

"No problem," I said. It's not like I had to be anywhere at any particular time. By now the kid had crawled under the bench and was grabbing at Muffin like he wanted to take her home with him. Fortunately his mother saw the bus coming and, still holding onto the kid's other hand, pulled him upright. Soldier and Princess scampered into the bus at the feet of the humans as they stepped inside through the front door.

"I guess we wait for the next one?" asked Muffin, as it was clear that the back door wasn't about to budge.

"But look," said Roscoe. "The kid is holding the door open." Sure enough, the little squirt had stopped in the doorway and was pointing toward us with the index finger of his free hand. He was babbling something in baby language that I took to mean, "Me want kitty," or something to that effect. His mother was rummaging through her purse for bus fare and was either not sympathetic to the child's desires, or more likely not conversant in baby language.

"Come on, let's go for it," I said. Without hesitation Roscoe and Muffin took off through the door like a couple of little furry rocket sleds, momentarily leaving me in the dust. I followed as quickly as I could and we joined the others undetected. Soldier nodded his appreciation for the bold move we had pulled off. I figured he wanted to be alone with Princess so I invited the kittens to roam around the bus with me. There's nothing more fun than watching a couple of them exploring a new environment. Muffin couldn't resist crawling into a lady's oversize handbag to steal a piece of chocolate. The human never even noticed, her full attention occupied by the little screen on the electronic device in her hands.

Soldier pulled the cord and the bell rang, signaling the driver to stop at the shopping mall. The five of us hopped out the back door. The bus sat there for a little while as the driver wondered why none of the humans on board were leaving. We had a good laugh as we scampered across the nearly-empty parking lot. Hiding behind the trash can next to the door of the fish and chips shop, we waited for the man to come outside for his cigarette break. I took the opportunity to tell my friends the details of my plan to provide the teenagers a place to congregate after school.

"What we'll do first is have the humans install a jukebox in the food court."

"A jukebox? What's that?" asked Soldier. "And how do you get them to do that?" He and Princess were peeking around the trash can hoping the door would open soon. Roscoe and Muffin had wandered off to a row of little bushes that grew along a blank wall of the shopping mall. They smelled mice.

"The jukebox provides the music so the kids can dance. It's a big machine full of these things called records. You put money in it and select which songs you want to hear."

"Sounds like something humans would do. And you're going to have them do this for you. How exactly?" Just then the door to the fish and chips shop opened and the fish and chips man propped the screen door wide open with a wooden crate. He proceeded to sit down on the crate and light up a cancer stick.

"I've got this," said Princess. She calmly stepped over to the human and began to slowly rub against his leg. I turned to Soldier and said, "Watch and learn, my friend." The human had only half way burned through his coffin nail when he picked her up and gently placed her in his lap. As he stroked Princess' silvery fur he seemed to stare off into the distance and become thoughtful.

"Yes, that's it," said the human softly. "A juke box in the food court. That will turn it around…"

Soldier looked at me with eyes wide. "How did she do that?"

"Focused purring," I said with a knowing grin. "I'll tell you all about it later, but right now I've got a hankering for some fish. Now where did those two kittens run off to?"

"Wait here," said Soldier. He darted over to the bushes and came back quickly with Roscoe and Muffin in tow. I could tell by the looks on their faces that they hadn't caught anything.

"Don't worry," I said. "There's fish in there! Follow me." I led the procession into the kitchen of the fish and chips shop, Princess jumping down off the human's lap to join us. He just sat there puffing on his cigarette appearing to be deep in thought. We snapped up whatever pieces of fish were to be found on the floor in no time. There wasn't enough to make much of a meal, though, there being five of us this time. Looking up, I spotted a basket of fish and chips sitting on the counter that had gone unclaimed. The teenage girl who worked there was sitting on her overturned five-gallon plastic drum, thumbs punching furiously at a little screen on the electronic device she held in her hands.

"Let's go!" I said, and hopped up on the counter, the others not hesitating to follow. We feasted on the fish and fries, even nibbling on the coleslaw which wasn't half bad. Soon we had finished it off and were hiding behind the trash can in the food court proper.

"Number forty-seven please, number forty-seven." The voice was that of the teenage girl in the fish and chips shop, who hadn't noticed that the basket on the counter was now empty. She sounded irritated. Apparently forty-seven was the number assigned to the purchaser of the large order of fish and chips (including coleslaw) who seemed to have been called away on business deemed more urgent than lunch. A cat would never abandon perfectly good fish but humans, well, they're a strange breed.

"Princess," I said, "why don't you show Soldier around the main part of the mall while I take the kittens down to the other end. I want to see how the mayoral campaign is coming along."
"Sounds good. Meet up here later?"
"That's a plan." I marched down to the little section of the shopping mall that extended out at a right angle to the main concourse. Nearly all of the store fronts here were empty. The entry way of the largest one was wide open and the display windows on either side were covered with *Bennett for Mayor* posters, banners, and stickers. I peeked in to see what was up. The kittens were busy amusing themselves by batting around an empty paper cup they had found. The place was full of humans, mostly middle aged to elderly women with a sprinkling of college students thrown in. They sat talking on phones, sealing papers in envelopes, removing other papers from other envelopes, darting back and forth, and gathering for little meetings. There was so much activity in the place that I grew weary just watching. Just as I was about to decide I'd seen enough I spotted two humans approaching. One was a tall man, impeccably dressed in a suit that was such a dark shade of blue that it may as well have been black. He wore a solid blue shirt and a plain red necktie, neatly tied. His haircut probably cost at least fifty dollars and a smile seemed to be stamped onto his face. The smile was more sinister than cheerful. A politician, no doubt. The other man was six inches shorter

and wore slacks and a sport coat. His haircut couldn't possibly have set him back more than twenty bucks. The shorter man walked a half step behind the politician. A politician's lackey, for sure.

I was about to round up the kittens and find a hiding place when two phones rang almost simultaneously in two coat pockets. The politician and his lackey each whipped out the little devices and became engaged in lively conversations. I relaxed, knowing that they would be oblivious to the presence of one cat and two kittens. When the tall man reached the *Bennett For Mayor* headquarters he barked, "Gotta go," and stuffed the phone back into his suit coat pocket. He simultaneously turned and shot the lackey a glance. The lackey ended his conversation without saying another word. By now Roscoe and Muffin had crept up behind me, the three of us peering into the storefront where things suddenly become interesting.

"Good afternoon, Ben." The politician extended his hand, a half-cheerful, half-sinister grin glued to his face. Ben Bennett immediately reached out and shook the man's hand. Each of the humans seemed to grimace a little, as if they were competing to see who had the firmer grip. The handshake continued for an uncomfortable length of time.

"Good afternoon," replied Mr. Bennett.

"So you're my opponent. What's the matter, car business not keeping you busy enough?"

"The car business is doing just fine, thank you very much."

"So is this all you've got?" The politician slowly turned his head to survey the room. The grin was now eighty-five percent sinister.

"Don't worry, we've got plenty."

The two exchanged pleasantries with insulting undertones for a while until the politician and his lackey turned to leave, the former muttering something about looking forward to Ben's concession speech. Ben Bennett stood there seething until Betty approached and grasped his upper arm with both hands. "Now honey, don't let that man get under your skin. We'll show him on Election Day." Ben didn't seem to hear her.

"Clarence!" The voice came from behind me, causing me to do a quick about face. Soldier and Princess had crept up behind us.

"Hey," I said, trying my best to not look surprised, "did you see that guy? He's running for mayor against my human."

"We've been eavesdropping on him down at the food court," said Princess. "Get this: the next mayor will be appointing the new dog catcher."

"Yeah, so?" I replied.

"So if this guy wins he's changing the title to *Animal Control Officer.*"

"Animal control? I don't like the sound of that."

"Yeah," said Soldier. "*Animals* includes us!"

"And he's a *dog person!*" Princess' words hung in the air like a thundercloud. We could all surmise what this meant. Lax enforcement of leash laws. Stray cats being rounded up for no particular reason. This was serious.

5) The Computer

The mood was subdued on our bus ride home, the possibility of a dog person in charge of "animal control" having put a big fat damper on the day. Soldier, Princess and I decided to visit Gramps and ask his advice as to how we should deal with this development. Roscoe and Muffin followed us. I got the feeling that they would be following us around a lot from now on. I didn't mind, though. Kittens are always good for some laughs. Have you ever seen one the first time they're around someone opening a can of tuna fish? *Hilarious!*

Gramps welcomed us all and showed us to a room at the far end of a hallway. The weather being pleasant, his human would certainly be away at the golf course all day. I took the room to be the library, the numerous shelves packed full of books being my first clue. It was rather dimly lit, the thick curtains on the only window being drawn shut. The walls were wood paneling all the way up to the ceiling and the floor was covered with plush maroon carpeting. Fancy lamps sat proudly upon ornate cabinets. Everything in the room seemed really, really old.

Gramps sat down on one of the plush chairs that were arranged around a table in the middle of the room. Princess, Soldier and I made ourselves comfortable on a sofa that faced the table. The sofa appeared to be a fairly new imitation of something really, really old.

"I'm glad you brought this to my attention," said Gramps gravely after we had explained the situation. "Something needs to be done," he added thoughtfully.

Meanwhile Roscoe and Muffin were chasing each other around the room as kittens will do.

"We've got to make sure that Clarence's human wins this election thing," said Soldier. This guy can sure restate the obvious, I thought, but I let it pass without comment.

"But what could we possibly do to help a human win an election?" asked Princess. "We can't vote. We're cats."

"You're forgetting," said Gramps slowly, "focused purring."

"Oh yeah. That."

"What are you suggesting?" I asked. "That we influence enough voters to vote for my human?"

"Sure, why not?"

"A couple of reasons," interjected Soldier. Aware of the look Gramps shot him, he added, "If you don't mind me saying, with all due respect..."

"Go on."

"There simply isn't enough time. Correct me if I'm wrong, but from what you've told me, in order for focused purring to work you've got to have the proper conditions. I mean, the human has to be settled down and not too distracted in order for a cat to curl up on its lap, right?"

"That's right."

"Well, to ensure that we've got enough votes we would have to influence hundreds, if not thousands of humans. Even if all six of us..."

"Four of us," said Gramps. He nodded towards the kittens as they flew by. "Those two are a little young for this."

"So four of us, even working night and day. Well, you do the math."

"You're right, Soldier. You're absolutely right."

"So what do we do?" said Princess.

Two thuds in rapid succession suddenly came from behind the sofa. The kittens had gotten carried away, running straight into the wall. I hopped up onto the back of the sofa to see that they had knocked a hole in the wood paneling. Not so much a hole as a doorway. A square piece of paneling, plenty big enough for an average human to crawl through, had swung inward on hinges to reveal a previously hidden room. Gramps quickly abandoned his chair, scurried to the opening, and crept inside.

"Wow, I never knew this was here!"

I followed him inside to find myself surrounded by piles of old books, newspapers and magazines. Roscoe and Muffin had climbed up onto one of the stacks and were playfully trying to push each other off. Soldier and Princess peered into the opening.

"Look at all this," said Gramps, who was already rummaging through the dusty old periodicals. "This is great. I finished all the books in the library years ago. It will be nice to have some fresh reading material."

"This stuff is really old," I said, noting the black-and-white photo on a weekly magazine.

"We can look at this stuff later," said Gramps as he stepped through the little doorway back into the library. I took the hint and followed him. "Right now we've got to figure out what to do about the election."

"I believe I have a solution," said Soldier.

"Do you? We'd love to hear it," said Gramps, taking his seat on the chair.

With a sly grin on his face, Soldier uttered a single word. "Sabotage!"

"I like the sound of that," replied Gramps. The newcomer had earned the respect of the old cat. "Do you have something specific in mind?"

"Oh yeah, I've got a plan. A good plan if I do say so myself."

After a pause that seemed longer than it was, Princess chimed in, "so are you going to tell us about it?"

"Better if I show you. Come on over to my place everyone." At this he bolted for the door. We followed, Gramps only remaining behind for a moment to carefully close the doorway to the secret room.

"I don't want my human throwing out any of those old magazines before I've had a chance to read them."

Princess and I followed on Soldier's heels as he led us around the corner and across the street to our block. Gramps and the kittens trailed behind a ways, which is a good thing. Half a dozen cats all walking together tends to get noticed by humans, and worse, by dogs. When we arrived at the back yard of his house I was wondering how we would get in since there was no pet door. Before I could say anything Soldier scampered up a tree and onto a limb that grew conveniently close to a window. He reached over and slid the window open with a paw.

"The latch has been broken for years," he chuckled as he disappeared into the house, "come on in. Don't worry, my human has a job, so he's gone all day." Three cats and two kittens followed enthusiastically, with only Gramps seeming a bit put out by having to climb the tree. Inside, a large desk was situated directly below the window.

"Oh boy, TV!" exclaimed Roscoe, referring to the screen that sat in the middle of the desk.

"Not exactly," said Soldier. "That's a monitor, and it's hooked up to a computer."

"Yeah," I said, "all the humans have them nowadays."

"Not mine," said Gramps.

"Look," said Soldier, "here's how you operate it; first hit the power switch, then use the keyboard and the mouse."

"Mouse? Did somebody say *mouse*?" Princess was licking her chops.

"Not that kind of mouse," said Soldier, pawing at the plastic thing next to the keyboard. "This thing here is called a *mouse* for some reason known only to humans."

"That doesn't look very appetizing."

"So we're going to sabotage the campaign with that thing." Gramps looked skeptical. "How?"

"Well, humans are now putting all the information that used to be in the newspaper online; news, gossip, advertising. All that stuff."

"Might explain why I haven't seen the paperboy in months," I interjected.

"Anyway," continued Soldier, "a politician running for office always has an official web site. That's where they publish information (and misinformation) meant to persuade people to vote for them. Here, I'll show you."

He proceeded to punch a few buttons here and there, then he started typing on the keyboard and fiddling with the *mouse* thingy. Some pictures and words appeared on the screen.

"Hey, that's me!" There was a photo of Ben, Betty and the kids, all dressed up and standing on the front lawn of the house. Mary Ann was holding me. Above the photo were big navy-blue letters spelling out *Ben Bennett For Mayor*. "I thought that picture was for the Christmas card."

"Probably was. Your buddy Max knows how to make interwebs so he created this site for his dad's campaign," said Soldier. "It's full of stories about what a fine upstanding citizen, family man and businessman he is."

"Wow, the kid's not as dumb as I thought. So where does it give Mr. B's positions on the issues?"

"Are you kidding? That's the last thing they want the voters to know. Take a stand on anything and half the people automatically hate you." Soldier then clicked the mouse thingy and banged on the keyboard a dozen or two times. "There it is: the opponent's web site. Substitute the names and photos and it's essentially the same as our guy."

"And this is what we're going to sabotage?" asked Gramps impatiently. "What are we going to do, trash their computer?"

"Hmmm... that's not a bad idea, but I had something else in mind. What if this web site was altered so that the guy doesn't look like such a fine upstanding citizen? Maybe some photos that aren't so flattering. Perhaps disclose some incidents in his past (real or imagined) that he'd rather no one know about."

"And some positions on the issues of the day, so half the people will hate him!" offered Princess.

"Better yet," said Muffin. It seems the youngsters were suddenly taking an interest in public affairs. "Some positions that are so outrageous that all but the clinically insane will hate him!"

"I like the way this kitty's mind works," said Soldier.

"So what are we waiting for? Let's do it!" asked Princess, pawing at the keyboard. After a brief silence she added, "So which button do we push?"

"Were it only that simple," sighed Soldier. "You can't just go in there and change a web site. You've got to have the password, and only the people who own the site have it. But we're going to get it."

"Focused purring?" This came out of the mouths of two or three of us.

"What else?"

"That could be tricky," I said. "The people running his campaign are surely dog people. They're not going to be very receptive, are they? Even if we can get them to let us sit on their laps."

"But are they all dog people? He hasn't taken a position on anything. There could be cat people working for the guy because they're convinced he's such a fine upstanding citizen. If we're lucky one of them knows the password. It's worth a try, isn't it?"

"I'm game."

"Sure, me too. Why not?"

"Great. I suggest two or three of us go to try and learn the password."

"Have fun," said Gramps as he got up to leave. "I'm going to go home to take a nap." By then we had exceeded the kittens' attention span. They had already gone out the window.

"I guess that leaves us three," I said. Hey, if Soldier can restate the obvious so can I.

"So where's this campaign headquarters?" asked Princess.

"Well, let's see. I'll just punch the address into the map site here."

"Wow, that's clear across town."

"Maybe the bus goes there," said Princess. "Can you get the schedules on this thing?"

"I can get anything on this thing," crowed Soldier. He seemed awfully pleased with himself, and who could blame him? "Let's see, according to the map here there's a route that goes right by there: number twenty-two."

"Perfect," I said. "We won't even have to transfer."

"We're gonna need to case the joint first." Soldier was suddenly talking like a crook in one of those old movies.

"Case the joint?"

"Yeah, you know, have a look around when there's nobody there. First we'll need to find out where the IT person sits. We want to use the closest possible entrance in order to minimize the chance of being seen."

"What's an IT person?" asked Princess.

"Information technology. Just fancy words for the computer guy. Or gal, but most of them seem to be guys.

Let's just hope ours is a cat person, or at least not a cat hater."

That evening we waited patiently for bus number twenty-two to arrive. The first one passed us by, but we got lucky when a young couple taking a stroll in the park took a seat on the bench. The bus stopped and the front door opened but the lovebirds didn't budge, the young man dismissing the bus driver with a wave of the hand. This of course provided plenty of time for Princess, Soldier and I to board.

"This bus is full of cats!" The voice belonged to a man who was half sitting and half lying on the seat just behind the driver. He had obviously had *one too many*, as the humans are fond of saying.

"I told you, if you don't pipe down you're walking the rest of the way home," said the driver wearily.

"Nice kitties..." whispered the inebriated man. Then he put his hands together to form a pillow, leaned over, and went to sleep. This was the one and only time I've seen a human passenger on a bus who *wasn't* clutching an electronic device in its hands.

There was no one else on the bus so we roamed around looking out the windows in various directions. Before long we were in territory that was new to me. I hope Soldier knows what he's doing, I thought.

"Here's the stop!" shouted Soldier, apparently suddenly realizing how far we had traveled. This of course was a serious breach of cat etiquette, since we're not supposed to talk loud enough around humans for them to hear us. If we all suddenly started talking out loud the humans would surely panic and run around in circles, screaming about the impending apocalypse, and forgetting to feed us in the process. This would be unacceptable.

"Here ya go," said the driver dryly as the bus wheezed to a stop and the doors opened. It seems he had mistaken Soldier's voice for the human's.

"Have a nice night," mumbled the inebriated one as he slowly made his way down the steps and out the front door. We took the opportunity to slip out the back door, then stood on the sidewalk waiting for the bus to pull away so we could cross the street to the campaign headquarters. Princess and I each gave Soldier a look.

"Okay, I'm sorry. I won't let it happen again."

"Well, no harm done I suppose," offered Princess.

The campaign headquarters was located in a one-story building that must have originally been a convenience store or video rental shop. The plate glass windows facing the street across a small parking lot were filled with campaign posters and banners, making it appear eerily similar to the Bennett headquarters. We dashed across the street, the traffic fortunately light this time of night. The front door was obviously shut tight and locked for the night, so we circled around to the back.

"I think I see a way in," I said. I hopped onto a dumpster that was situated right against the back wall of the building. Standing on my hind legs and stretching, I was able to reach a vent covering and wiggle it loose. The rectangular piece of metal made a clanging sound as it bounced off of the dumpster and onto the pavement. A dog across the alley barked. "Come on in," I said with delight.

"Good work," said Soldier as he and princess followed me inside. We only had to creep a few feet before finding a ceiling vent that was conveniently located above a desk. One by one we dropped down onto the jumbled stacks of paper that covered the surface of the desk. We probably made a mess of things, but something told me that the human who would sit here the next morning would hardly notice. "Now, where oh where is the IT guy?"

"Or gal," added Princess.

"Yeah," I said, "how will we know which desk it is?"

"It's usually the one with the big paper coffee cups. And lots of science fiction movie paraphernalia such as action figures and robots."

"Over there!" Princess was pointing to the corner of the room with her paw.

6) The Taxicab

"This is too easy," said Soldier with a laugh. He had flipped over the keyboard to find a scrap of paper taped to the underside. "Login password and web server password, right here for the taking." We immediately committed them to memory, which was not difficult at all considering that they were *password1* and *password2*. "Humans. You gotta love 'em!" said Soldier as he flipped the keyboard over again and began punching keys with both paws.

"Are we going to sabotage now?" asked Princess, staring at the screen.

"No, I'm just going to get the web address for the server. We don't need to hang around here any longer than necessary." He continued to punch keys and click that thing that the humans insist on calling a *mouse*. "That's an awfully long address. We'll need to put it on paper so I won't have to try and remember it."

"How do you propose to accomplish that?" I asked, "Last time I checked writing required the use of opposable thumbs, which none of us have."

"Easy peasy." He punched at the keyboard for a while and then made a big show of dramatically pressing one last key. A plastic box on the corner of the desk whirred to life. After a moment it spit out a sheet of paper. Soldier took the sheet in his paws and carefully tore off the part with the relevant information with his teeth.

"I'm glad you're on our side," was all I could manage to say.

In order to get out of the place we returned to the other desk. It took the strength of all three of us, but we managed to move the computer monitor onto a big stack of paper. One after another we climbed and pulled ourselves up into the ceiling vent. The human would surely wonder how his computer monitor got onto the stack of paper, but hey, what did we care? We got outside to find that the dog had stopped barking. Just for fun I let out a loud meow in order to get him going again. A human was standing at the stop for the bus heading back home. I recognized him as the man on the bus, the one who had obviously had *one too many*. Another man walked by briskly with his hands in his pockets.

"Excuse me, sir," said the man from the bus, "could you call me a cab?"

"You're a cab," said the other man without breaking stride.

"Good one. I'm a cab!" he laughed. Then he turned toward the street, pointing a finger in the air and shouting *"TAXI!"* to every vehicle that passed by. Eventually a bright yellow car pulled over and came to a stop. The man opened the back door and held on to it for a moment so as not to lose his balance, giving us plenty of time to hop aboard. The address he gave the driver could have been anywhere for all we knew.

"We need to go downtown," whispered Soldier. "Two-Ten Maple Street, okay?"

"No sweat," said Princess. She gently climbed onto the passenger's lap and was soon purring contentedly.

"Driver, never mind that. Take me downtown. I just remembered, I've got to go downtown! Two-Ten Maple Street."

"Two-Ten Maple Street it is." The driver didn't seem to consider the change of destination the least bit odd. I kept quiet as did Princess, both of us now confident that Soldier knew what he was doing. After a brief ride that included some rather sudden turns that nearly toppled the human passenger, the taxicab screeched to a halt. We darted out of the car the instant the back door opened and watched the man slowly get out of the car, stagger over to the driver's side window and pay the cabbie. After the taxicab drove away he just stood there on the curb scratching his head.

"What the- I don't live here... hey, nice kitties..."

I found myself looking up at an impressive-looking building complete with columns and wide steps leading up to an entrance that consisted of several big metal doors side by side. Carved in the stonework above the entrance were the words *Public Library*.

"Suddenly have the urge to check out a book or two?" asked Princess.

"Books? Nope, we're going to use the computer here. This way the sabotage can't be traced back to our humans."

"Good thinking," I had to say.

We slipped inside just before closing time and found a computer terminal off in a side room with no humans around. Soldier sat down in front of the screen with

Princess and me on either side. He spit out the piece of paper he had been carrying in his mouth and pounded away on the keyboard that sat in front of the computer monitor.

"Okay, we're in! Now, first I'll change the password, let's see, something easy to remember... *catnip*. Now we come up with a phony press release that makes the guy look totally clueless. Any suggestions?"

"I know," said Princess, "let's have him propose installing pogo stick lanes on all major arteries throughout the city."

"Brilliant," I said. Soldier resumed his pounding on the keyboard. "I've got one. He wants to change the name of the city, maybe name it after one of his kids or his dog."

"I like it, I like it."

"Clothing-optional Fridays for all City employees!" squealed Princess.

"Okay, okay," said Soldier, laughing, "hold that thought until I get caught up."

"How about he proposes using city funds to pay for a memorial to the unknown cow," I offered.

By the time an hour had passed we had crafted what surely had to rank as one of the most embarrassing documents in the history of politics. Soldier then set up a bogus e-mail account and proceeded to send a copy to all the local newspapers and radio and television stations. Our work done here, we roamed around the now empty library looking for a way out. I spotted an exit sign off in a corner and we went over to discover a door marked *EMERGENCY EXIT ONLY*. An aluminum bar was attached horizontally across the door, just out of reach. I stepped back and took a running start, easily leaping high enough to hit the bar and fling the door open. Instantly a very loud bell started ringing and a red light on the outside of the building began to flash on and off. We took off running, laughing all the way. In fact our kitty adrenaline was so high that we didn't even try to catch a ride home and gladly walked all the way.

June came and with it Mary Ann's graduation from high school. This of course meant that the Bennetts would throw another party. All of her classmates were also entertaining at their own homes, leaving the number of available guests at practically zero. Other than the immediate family, only Aunt Martha, Pete, and one of Mary Ann's friends, the brunette, were present. So even though it was a Saturday night and school was out for the summer, it wasn't much of a party. After everyone, including the cats of course, had partaken of cake and punch, the humans drifted off into various rooms. Max and Joey were soon playing a video game on the TV in the den. Mary Ann, Pete and her friend went outside and Princess and I followed. Ben Bennett excused himself and drove off to meet with someone or other at campaign headquarters.

The humans took their places on the lawn furniture on the patio, Mary Ann and her boyfriend on the metal sofa with waterproof cushions and the brunette friend on a folding chair. The sofa seemed to rock back and forth a bit, but whether it was by design or a result of wear and tear I couldn't say.

"So what's everyone gonna do now?" asked the brunette while absent mindedly twirling some of her hair around an index finger.

"Call it a night, I suppose, unless there's anything good on TV," replied the boyfriend.

"No, not now as in tonight. Now as in what are you gonna do with your life? And I meant Mary Ann. You already graduated a year ago and are still stuck at that ice cream parlor."

"I'll have you know the company has a management training program, and next month I'll be eligible to apply. If I get in they'll pay for my business classes at the junior college. The sky's the limit in the ice cream business. It's a national chain, you know." The brunette didn't seem to be particularly impressed.

"And what about you, girl?" said Mary Ann.

"I don't know, my parents want me to go to college right away."

"Try not to burst from enthusiasm," sneered Pete.

"I'm sorry, I just can't get too excited about more school. Counting kindergarten I've just finished thirteen years' worth. I think my brain is full."

"So are you going to get a job or just leech off of your parents?" asked Mary Ann's boyfriend. He and the brunette had started up an informal game of *catch* with a little rubber ball.

"Well, I wasn't going to say anything, but..."

"But what?"

"I've applied to be a flight attendant," she said with an embarrassed grin. The game of catch picked up a little speed at this point. "If I get in I go to LA for training, then I'd be based there or Dallas or maybe Atlanta." A mixture of surprise and disappointment appeared on the face of Mary Ann at this revelation. Her friend immediately added, "Don't worry, I'll be back to visit all the time. Free flights on my days off, you know. Besides, once I work my way up to the first class cabin I'll catch me a rich man and be his trophy wife!"

"Not if you don't do something with your hair," said the boyfriend, astutely dodging the fastball that was launched at his head as a result of the remark.

"So what about you, babe? You've been totally secretive about your plans."

"I've applied to a college," said Mary Ann, "but I'm not saying anything so as not to jinx it."

"No fair. We told you our plans, now spit it out."

"Okay, but don't tell anyone else. My grades were good, but for this program they're probably not good enough. If I don't get in, I'd just as soon nobody knows about it, okay?" The other two nodded. "I applied to the technical institute, the one up north."

"Really?" said the boyfriend. "Isn't that for Brainiac only?"

"Like I said, I probably won't get in. But if I do I want to be a rocket scientist."

"Cool," said the brunette. "I'll be rich, you'll be famous, and that guy can get us free ice cream cones. Life is good."

7) The Jukebox

July arrived and with it a heat wave, so most days I was staying inside to take advantage of the air conditioning. One day Betty Bennett and Aunt Martha were sitting on the couch in the living room. I had a feeling there would be something interesting discussed and curled up at their feet.

"What's wrong, Betty? You look worried. Is everything all right?"

"Oh Martha," she sighed, "does it show? It's Ben's business. He's afraid they're going to be audited."

"Audited? That's not a good thing, is it?"

"Not at all. The manufacturer is undergoing a tax audit and from what they've told Ben their offices are crawling with revenue agents."

"But he doesn't work for the manufacturer. He's his own boss, isn't he?" Martha took Betty's right hand in her left.

"I'm afraid they'll be selecting some of the dealerships for audit, too. And since Ben's a sole proprietor they can look at all of our finances. Not that we have anything to worry about, at least I don't think we have anything to worry about. I'm not looking forward to it, though, having some stranger looking through all of our papers."

"When will you find out?"

"Any day now. The notifications are supposedly already in the mail."

That afternoon Mary Ann and her friends, the blonde and the brunette, borrowed Mrs. Bennett's car to go shopping. They returned a few hours later, each carrying a shopping bag, and went directly to Mary Ann's room. Curious as always, I followed at their heels, hopped onto the bed, and curled up on a pillow. Due to the chattering and laughing of the girls, Princess awoke from the nap she was taking on a chair. The girls emptied out the shopping bags, the contents of which were various items of used clothing. I jumped off the bed and moved to a spot in the corner of the room so as to avoid being buried.

Someone knocked five times on the bedroom door but the girls either didn't hear it or chose to ignore it. The piles of clothes on the bed had their undivided attention. The three of them were holding blouses and pants up against themselves the way women do when they want to evaluate multiple garments without taking the time to try them on. The knocking resumed, this time much louder.

"Mary Ann! Open up!" could be heard through the closed door. The voice was that of Max, Mary Ann's brother. "Did you borrow my racket again?" The emphasis he placed on the word *borrow* seemed to indicate a healthy dose of sarcasm.

"Oh, all right," said Mary Ann. "Come in." Without having to be asked, the brunette friend, being closest to the door, reached around and pulled it open without taking her eyes off of the used clothing.

"Whoa, what's all this?" Max surveyed the scene with a half grin on his face.

"None of your business," snapped the brunette. She tossed him the tennis racket that Mary Ann had just handed her. Max caught it with one hand. The blonde turned towards him just long enough to shoot him an icy glance.

"Are you actually going to wear those skirts?" Max laughed, oblivious to the hostility of his sister's friends. "That is so lame. What did you do, dig up a time capsule from nineteen seventy-nine?"

"They're *dresses*, not skirts, weirdo." Mary Ann actually liked her little brother but caved to peer pressure when her friends were around and made sure to toss him a halfhearted insult or two. "And they're *cool!*"

"Yeah, cooler than you'll ever be," said the blonde.

"Way cool," added the brunette quite unnecessarily.

"Okay, I know I'm not the hippest dude by a long shot but really, this crap went out of style twenty years ago. Not cool. Where did you even find this stuff? You're not going to wear it to school are you?"

"Don't you get it?" said the blonde. "Of course it's not cool. It's thoroughly lame, old-fashioned, outdated and hideously ugly. But it's so out of date that it's cool again, *retro cool!*"

"We found it at that second-hand store downtown," added the brunette. "You know, where the department store used to be."

"And yes," said Mary Ann, not about to be left out, "we're wearing it to school Monday. That way we can go straight to the food court after school."

"The food court?"

"Yeah, haven't you been to Pinewood lately?" asked Mary Ann. "They put in a jukebox at the food court. A big old thing full of forty-five r.p.m. records, all of them dance music from the seventies."

"They've got the lights dimmed and they hung up one of those mirrored balls from the ceiling, the kind that spins around," said the blonde excitedly. She seemed to have forgotten that she was supposed to be mean to Max.

"They wanted to have the dance floor light up in all different colors," added the brunette in a downright friendly tone, "but it was too expensive so they just painted colored squares on the floor."

"It's great," said Mary Ann. "Now we have a place to go after school."

"So they did all this to get a bunch of teenagers to hang out at the mall," said Max. "Why?"

"I guess the place was so dead they were desperate to get warm bodies in there. I dunno, maybe they figure our parents will go inside and buy something when they drop us off."

At that moment Mary Ann's boyfriend Pete literally danced into the room.

"Peetie! You look great!" I would have had to agree if by *great* she meant ridiculous. The young man was wearing white bell-bottom slacks, a loosely fitting brightly colored V-neck silk shirt, patent leather boots, and an oversize medallion hanging on a gold chain around his neck.

"Wow, that's soooo bad," squealed the blonde. From previous experience I knew that *bad* could often mean *good* depending on the context. Don't ask me why.

"Bitchin'," said the brunette. This too I interpreted as a good thing.

"So get changed," said Pete, "and we'll go to the food court." This was clearly directed to Mary Ann, but the other two girls took it to mean they were invited.

"Yeah, let's go," they said simultaneously.

"Okay," said Mary Ann, "we'll meet you there." I recalled that Pete drove one of those little sports cars with no back seat. This meant that the blonde and the brunette would be driving in a separate car. When Pete stepped out of the room to allow the girls to change clothes I followed. Just because I'm a cat doesn't mean I'm not a gentleman. The glances Princess and I exchanged let us both know that we were thinking the same thing, that is, we would hitch a ride with the two girls. This was something we had to see for ourselves, this *disco food court*.

Princess and I easily sneaked into the back seat of the blonde's little two-door car. The two girls followed Mary Ann and Max to the Pinewood Mall and met up at the main entrance. It was quite a sight, Max in his bell bottoms and the girls in their frilly chiffon dresses in pastel colors. Mary Ann wore blue of course, the blonde green, the brunette yellow. They had parked the car directly in front of the main entrance, but Princess and I opted to circle around and enter through the fish and chips shop. The door was closed so we sat down to wait for the fish and chips man to come outside for his cigarette break.

"Nice kitties." We were so intent on watching the door that we hadn't noticed the approach of a human. That's something you don't see every day, a human sneaking up on cats. A man carrying a box labeled *Friedle's Frozen French Fries* in his left hand approached the door and pulled a key chain loaded with keys out of his pants pocket. This was a different fish and chips man, younger and better groomed. He carefully unlocked the door and opened it just enough to allow himself and the box to enter. Princess and I were about to follow him inside when he turned and stuck out his foot.

"Oh no you don't," he said, "not with the health inspector due today." The door slammed.

"This is no good," said Princess. "I want some fish." She seemed to have picked up Soldier's penchant for restating the obvious.

"Come on," I said, "let's go in through the main entrance." We didn't have to wait long for a door to swing open. The woman who appeared was holding a paper shopping bag with a department store logo imprinted across the entire side. The bag was so large she could barely see where she was going, allowing us to stroll across the threshold undetected. Evidence of the transformation of the food court into a disco dance hall was evident from just inside the entrance. We could hear the thumping of bass notes and vague sounds of voices chattering away. It sounded like a party. Princess and I hurried along past the store fronts, stopping to hide behind a trash can when some humans approached from the other direction.

When we reached the food court we stopped and peeked around the corner. The tables had all been moved so as to leave the center of the room open. Sure enough, the floor in the middle had been painted in colored squares in a feeble attempt to mimic the embedded flashing lights that were so popular back in the disco era. The music was genuine, though, as one of the hottest dance tunes from nineteen seventy-seven blasted from the vintage Wurlitzer. The juke box had colored lights that actually flashed off and on, although the purple bulb needed replacing. The crowd was entirely made up of teenagers, roughly half of them decked out in disco-era clothing. The others were in their usual school clothes, except for one very embarrassed boy who had, for one reason or another, showed up in a three-piece suit. Several couples were dancing, but with little or no consensus as to the moves. Some were slow-dancing together, others fast-dancing apart, apparently making it up as they went along. One couple was showing off with twirls and dips that bore no relation whatsoever to the tempo of the music. The whole scene was engulfed in bits of light from a mirrored ball suspended from the ceiling that swam across the room like a school of little luminescent fish.

Princess and I just stood there for a while staring at the bizarre scene in front of us.

"What have we done?" I murmured.

"Hey, the kids have somewhere to go after school. That's what we wanted, right?"

"I guess. At least it will be easy to get into the fish and chips shop without being seen."

Not requiring any further encouragement, Princess darted across the room. I followed, and we jumped over the counter. The girl who worked there had exchanged her fast-food uniform for a colorful blouse and a pair of denim bell bottoms. She was too busy watching the dance floor to notice us. To our surprise and disappointment, the place had been thoroughly cleaned since our last visit. Everything from the deep fryers to the walk-in refrigerator door was polished just as shiny as new. Anything that wasn't currently in use had been neatly hung up, put away, or discarded. Worst of all, the floor was spotless. Not a scrap of fish or fry to be found.

"Ain't that the way of the world?" I said. "Just when something gets good, there's somebody there to ruin it for you."

The next day I was just about to settle down to take a nap in the living room when I saw Betty Bennett enter the room. She was holding the stack of envelopes and magazines that constituted the day's mail in her left hand, flipping through it with the index finger of her right. Not seeing any reason to be particularly interested, I curled up and closed my eyes. Seconds later my nap, if you could call it that, came to an abrupt end as a shriek filled the room. The various pieces of U.S. Mail soared upward briefly and then fell to the floor to form a circle around Mrs. Bennett.

"What's wrong?" cried an anxious-looking Mary Ann as she ran into the room.

"Just what your father and I were afraid of, dear. We're being audited." She knelt down and picked up an envelope and handed it to Mary Ann. The letters *IRS* were clearly visible above the return address in the upper left-hand corner.

"Relax, Mom, this is addressed to me."

"You're being audited?"

"Don't be silly. This is from the college I applied to, the Institute of Rocket Science," said Mary Ann, her voice rising to a crescendo. She tore open the envelope and fished out a single page. "Whee! I got in!" she squealed, quite literally jumping for joy.

"The institute of *what*?"

"I wasn't going to say anything, in case I didn't get in. My grades are good after all, but I mean, hey, it's rocket science!"

"Oh, my baby's going to be a rocket scientist!" said Betty, placing her palms on her daughter's cheeks. "Gimme a hug!"

8) The Charity Ball

A couple of weeks later Ben and Betty were sitting in the den with the television on, although they didn't seem to be watching it. Their children were all occupied elsewhere; Mary Ann in her room chatting with a friend on the phone, Max out running around with a couple of his buddies, and Joey in the back yard repeatedly tossing a ball against the wall in the midsummer evening sun. I had just hopped up onto Betty's lap in order to have the channel changed to Animal Planet. By now I was skilled enough at focused purring to have my choice of TV shows any time I wanted. Before I could get comfortable Mr. Bennett dropped a bombshell on his wife. I'm speaking figuratively of course.

"What do you mean *the dealership is losing money*?"

"I mean it's losing money," said Ben, "as in paying out more than it's taking in. Simple, really." He was leaning forward with elbows on knees, his fingertips rubbing his temples.

"But why, dear?" Betty had one of those looks humans get on their faces when they don't quite comprehend what's going on. "It's always made money before."

"Things change. Our sales are way down what with that new lot down the street selling those sweet little imports that everybody wants nowadays. With all the time I've been spending on the campaign, I've had to delegate approving deals to one of the sales people. I haven't had time to look into it, but I suspect cars are selling at a loss just for the commissions. And it doesn't help that we've kept practically the same staff as before. I just hate letting people go. It all adds up to some big time negative cash flow."

"What about Mary Ann?" she asked as she stood up, gently plopping me onto the floor. "You've already promised her she could start at the rocket scientist school in the fall. How are we going to afford it?"

"She'll have to apply for financial aid, I suppose."

"Nope," said Betty, "she already tried that. We're too rich to qualify, at least this year anyway."

"How about a scholarship? She's always had good grades."

"They're good enough for her to get accepted, but not good enough for a scholarship, not at the rocket science institute. Do you have any idea how competitive it is?"

Ben, seemingly dismissing this as a rhetorical question, said, "I guess she'll have to go to junior college, at least until things turn around."

"I need to start getting ready for tonight. Remember, Ben, you promised you would take me to the foul ball this year." Foul ball? Wasn't that a baseball term? This seemed odd, Mrs. Bennett not being much of a sports fan. Betty was holding up something that resembled a greeting card like a soccer referee indicating a booking. She dropped the document on the coffee table and then marched toward the master bedroom without another word. I waltzed over to the coffee table, pushed up with my hind legs and rested my front paws on the tabletop. The card said:

The Seventh Annual Fowl Ball
All proceeds go to preservation of wetlands and waterfowl
habitat
7:00pm until Midnight

The rest of the stylized lettering gave the date and the address of the venue. Now that I could see that it was f-o-w-l and not f-o-u-l it made sense. Animal planet insisted on showing some nonsense about dogs so I got bored and wandered into Mary Ann's room to eavesdrop on the phone conversation. By now she had finished talking to her friend and was having a lively discussion with the boyfriend.

"Work? What do you mean you have to work? Peetie, you promised!" said Mary Ann, her voice a notch higher on the treble clef than usual. Even with my excellent cat hearing I couldn't quite make out Pete's response.

"How do you expect me to go to a ball without a date?" Then Pete said something.

"Oh yeah? I'll get a date, just watch me!" With this she took the phone away from her ear and savagely punched a button, presumably ending the connection. "What am I saying? I can't get a date on an hour's notice." Then she picked me up and announced to no one in particular, "Clarence will be my date. I'm taking Clarence to the Fowl Ball!"

I politely retired into the den while Mary Ann changed into her black strapless evening gown. When she made her entrance into the living room her parents were rather vocal in their praise. No doubt had Pete seen her in that outfit he would have walked off the job, escorted her to the ball, and worried about seeking employment another day. Suited me fine to take his place. Mary Ann was the only one of the Bennett kids to accompany Ben and Betty to the Fowl Ball, Max having been recruited to stay home that evening with Joey. Princess would surely have wanted to come along, but she had left earlier to go down to Soldier's house. They had plans to go out tree climbing.

Mary Ann picked me up and carried me across the living room toward the front door.

"What are you doing? You'll get cat hair all over your dress." said Betty.

"He's my date. My former boyfriend Pete stood me up, so I'm taking Clarence to the ball. I'm going to tell everybody what a jerk he is." I trusted the last part referred to Pete, not me.

"Well, the tickets don't say anything about not bringing cats, so I guess it's all right."

Ben opened the passenger side door of the two-door car and pushed the seat forward so that Mary Ann and I could get in the back seat. Just then Betty said she had forgotten something and started back towards the house, but stopped when Ben volunteered to retrieve the item. At that moment two flashes of fur came flying into the car. Roscoe and Muffin scampered past Mary Ann's legs and made themselves comfortable on the floor in front of the unoccupied seat. Mary Ann, between holding me and fiddling with her seat belt, didn't seem to notice them. My little friends had executed a one-door tag-along!

Betty pushed the front seat back into place with a thump.

"Mom, could you move it forward a bit? The seat is right against my knees. I feel like I'm on a discount airline."

"Sorry, dear." The seat scooted up a few inches and Betty sat down.

The Fowl Ball was being held in the Grand Ballroom of the Royal Lion Hotel downtown. Nice, I thought, have a thing for the birds at a joint named for a cat. The Grand Ballroom turned out to be Meeting Rooms A, B, and C, partitions A-B and B-C having been temporarily removed. *Grand* is not the first word that would come to mind if I were asked to describe the place. Tables of various shapes and sizes were placed haphazardly around the combined rooms. I noted three different styles of chairs, but gave the organizers credit for arranging them in one and only one style per table. A makeshift bandstand was set up against the far wall of Room B. It was only about a foot in height, the acoustic ceiling panels hanging too low to allow anything more. A poster board with cursive writing in green glitter announced the evening's music as being provided by The Cool Cucumbers Jazz Orchestra. The musicians were attired in white slacks, black shoes, white shirts, black bow-ties, and matching green sport coats. From the looks of them I guessed their average age to be approximately eighty-three years.

We were apparently early, as only a few couples had claimed seats at the various tables. The Bennetts chose one near the bandstand, a round table that seated eight.

Mary Ann deposited me on the chair next to her. Roscoe and Muffin had scampered in undetected and took up residence just in front of Mary Ann's toes. Little by little the chairs at the various tables became populated with humans. Whenever someone walking by or taking their place at a nearby table noticed me, Mary Ann would declare, "Yes, this cat is my date. My stupid jerk ex-boyfriend Pete stood me up!" You know what they say about a woman scorned.

The remaining places at our table were soon filled by Mary Ann's friends, the blonde and the brunette, escorted by identical twins. The young men were tall and lanky with red hair and freckles. Their sport coats were a growth spurt away from obsolescence and I got the distinct impression that it was perhaps the third occasion in each of their lives that required the tying of a necktie.

"What's the cat doing here?" asked the brunette as she took a seat next to me.

"Clarence is my date because my stupid jerk ex-boyfriend Pete stood me up!"

"Well I never thought you and Pete would last. I mean, really, you can do better. In fact," she continued, looking at me, "you may already have." Can't argue with that.

Once more or less everyone had taken their seats, waiters and waitresses dressed in red and black spread out among the tables in a benign invasion. The gangly young man assigned to our table politely asked each human what they would like to drink and whether they would prefer an entree of chicken or fish.

"Iced tea and chicken," said Mary Ann. I let out a loud meow. "Make that fish." The waiter must have been a cat person, or more likely he found Mary Ann attractive, because when dinner was served he brought her the chicken dinner and set a small plate with a big fat piece of grilled sole in front of me. Of course I discreetly shared some with the kittens.

After dinner, the band struck up a lively tune and the humans took to the dance floor, The Bennetts, the blonde, the brunette, and their redheaded escorts included. Eight bars later a young man asked Mary Ann to dance. I'm pretty sure it was the waiter in a borrowed sport coat. Roscoe and Muffin took this as their cue to climb up onto the table and see what kind of mischief they could produce. I was feeling much too lazy to join in, so I curled up on my chair to digest my fish and listen to the music. It turns out one or two of those geezers could blow a pretty mean horn after all. After the fifth tune the band needed a breather so the seven humans once again took their seats around the table.

"Hey," squealed the blonde, "there's a picture of a kitten's face on my phone!"

"Same here," said the first redheaded escort.

"Who called Barcelona on my phone?" The second redheaded escort looked accusingly around the room.

"Somebody ordered seventy-five dollars' worth of cat toys on my phone!" And on it went. Roscoe and Muffin, of course, were by this time rolling around on the floor under the table. It was all they could do to keep their squeaky little kitten laughs from being heard by the humans.

9) The Magazine

The next day Princess and I were hanging around on the front porch when Joey's little friend came over to visit. He shuffled up the walk carrying a puppy in his arms. Normally cats would take exception to seeing a canine enter our territory. This mutt, though, was so tiny and pathetic that we just couldn't be bothered. The kid rang the doorbell and Mrs. Bennett let him in and sent him and the dog to Joey's room.

"Too bad about Mary Ann not being able to go to rocket science school," said Princess.

"Yes, I keep thinking there's got to be a way. Maybe we could hitch a ride there and try some focused purring."

"But it's a long way away, isn't it? We don't even know where it is."

"True," I said, straining my little cat brain to come up with something. "We'll have to talk to Soldier. Maybe he'll have an idea."

Just then the front door flew open and the puppy bounded out. Apparently Joey and his friend had been playing "dress-up" with the poor critter. A brightly colored Hawai'ian shirt had been awkwardly draped around its torso, a red bandana tied around its neck, and a straw hat stuck on top of its tiny head. The hat was held in place by ears protruding through two holes that seemed to have been freshly cut for that purpose. For a finishing touch, the boys had fastened around the mutt's neck a necklace, which I recognized as one that Joey had presented to Mary Ann at her birthday party back in May.

For the first time in my lives I found myself feeling sorry for a dog.

The puppy didn't stop when it reached the front yard, oh no, it kept right on running into the street and off into the distance. Joey and his friend ran out after the dog but came to a screeching halt at the sidewalk, their mothers having told them in no uncertain terms to never, ever play in the street. After standing there helplessly for a minute or two the two boys were slowly walking back towards the house, when a truck went by headed in the opposite direction from where the puppy had run. On the side of the truck was painted *Route 58 Trading Post*, and peeking out of the back was a furry little head wearing a straw hat, a red bandana, and a necklace with a red gemstone. Princess and I just laughed and laughed.

We were still laughing when Gramps arrived. In his mouth was a folded-up sheet of paper which he dropped onto the porch. "What's so funny?"

"You should have seen it, Gramps," said Princess. "Those human boys dressed a dog up in silly clothes and then it ran off and hitched a ride on a truck."

"Well that sounds like great fun, but look here. I've got something important to show you. Remember that secret closet, the one with all the old books and magazines? Look at what I found in there." Gramps unfolded the paper, which was a page he had torn out of one of the old magazines. There was a color photograph of a rather well dressed middle aged couple posing by an airplane in front of a hanger. Spelled out in black block lettering above the hangar doors was *DuRauque Aviation*. A caption read *Wealthy Industrialist and Wife To Attempt*

Round-The-World Flight. Gramps flipped over the page to show us the other side, which contained a close-up photograph of the lady in the other picture and the first few paragraphs of an article.

"There it is!" he said, "does that look familiar?"

"Wow," said Princess, looking over my shoulder.

"Mary Ann's ruby?"

"The one and only," said Gramps. "The article says that the ruby necklace is a priceless family heirloom with tremendous sentimental value. It disappeared shortly after the photo was taken. Despite offering a substantial reward, it was never recovered. And fifty years later it shows up at Mary Ann's birthday party. I bet the rich folks would pay a bundle to get it back."

"One problem," I said. "It's gone."

"Gone?" said Gramps. "What do you mean, *gone*?"

"Gone," I said. "As in no longer here. That puppy was wearing it, and *he's* gone, apparently on his way to the Route 58 Trading Post. We didn't think anything of it, you know, believing the ruby to be a cheap imitation. We've got to get it back." It was my turn to restate the obvious.

"I'll go get Soldier. He'll know what to do," said Princess as she scampered away.

"We need to get a ride to the trading post, that's what we need," said Gramps, but by then she was out of earshot.

Gramps and I went inside in hopes of finding a target for some focused purring. Other than Joey and his friend, Betty Bennett was the only one home. She was engaged in a lively conversation on the phone, something about the occurrence of a crisis at campaign headquarters. The two boys were tugging on her skirt and whining about the dog's escape, but made no impression on the lady. Our attention was diverted by the sound of an automobile horn coming from the street in front of the house. We darted outside to see what was up and found Aunt Martha disembarking from a shiny new car, the sticker still in the side window and a piece of paper in the rear window in lieu of license plates.

"Betty! O, Betty! Look what I've bought!" she proclaimed repeatedly as she marched across the front lawn and into the house.

"What's going on?" The voice was Soldier's, he and Princess having just arrived with Roscoe and Muffin in tow.

"It seems Aunt Martha has bought a car," I said.

"Great, she can take us to the trading post."

"No way. I've seen the way she drives."

"No problem," said Gramps. "We'll drive it ourselves!"

"Are you kidding?" exclaimed Princess. "How can we do that?"

"Teamwork, my friends. Teamwork."

At that point I realized that Aunt Martha had left the driver's side door wide open. Not only that, but the keys were in the ignition and the motor was still running. With Gramps leading the way, half a dozen cats sprang into action. We piled into the car, each taking our positions according to Gramps' directions. Princess took the gas pedal with Roscoe and Muffin jointly in charge of the brake pedal. I had the honor of steering the thing, which I would do by alternately pressing my paws downward on the horizontal bar inside the steering wheel. Nine o'clock for a left turn and three o'clock for a right.

"You'll be in charge of the perndle," said Gramps to Soldier.

"Right. The perndle. Umm... what's a perndle?"

"See that thing with the handle there in the middle? The P is for park, R is for reverse, N for neutral, D for drive and L for low gear. P-R-N-D-L. *Perndle!*"

"Perndle. Got it."

Gramps took up his position as navigator by standing up on his hind legs on the passenger seat with his paws on the dashboard.

Princess leaned on the gas pedal, the sudden acceleration taking me by surprise. I had to push down hard with my left paw to avoid the car that was parked on the street in front of the house next door to the Bennetts. Before I could straighten the wheel, the path of the car took us straight into a mailbox on the other side of the street. The box and the wood pole that supported it went down and I could hear crunching and clanging as the car ran over them, leaving behind a flattened mailbox, several pieces of mail strewn about, and the pole reduced to firewood.

"Easy, Princess!" exclaimed Gramps, "you gotta accelerate smoothly, don't just stomp on it."

"Sorry about that."

We managed to get to the end of the street and hang a left on Maple, which took us to the highway. Along the way two more mailboxes and a newspaper vending machine were added to the casualty list.

"Ease off the gas Princess, and you two lean on that brake pedal." Soldier, Gramps and I were relieved to see that we had stopped in time to avoid being T-boned by the traffic on Route 58.

"Okay, Clarence, get ready to make a hard right. Ready on the gas Princess... *NOW!*"

The car fishtailed (did someone say fish?) onto the highway and accelerated. I steered left and right to avoid the cars we were passing like they were standing still. Once we got out of the city limits the traffic thinned out and I could take my eyes off of the road long enough to have a look at the speedometer. Seventy in a fifty-five zone, not good. I was just about to ask whoever was meowing to pipe down when the flashing lights in the rear-view mirror told me that what I was hearing was not one of my compatriots, but the siren of a police car.

"Keep going," shouted Gramps, "we're almost there."

"Hit the brakes, kids, hit the brakes!" I yelled as we approached the *Route 58 Trading Post* sign. Roscoe and Muffin were laughing too hard to have heard me, but Soldier alertly pounced on the brake pedal. The tires squealed and kicked up a cloud of dust in the unpaved parking lot. The passenger side door flew open as we plowed into the side of the stone-and-mortar building. The six of us scampered out of the car, unseen by the police officers due to the cloud of steam spewing forth from the broken radiator. We circled around to the back of the building to catch our breath behind a dumpster. Peeking around the corner I could see the two officers peering into the driver's side door of Aunt Martha's car, no doubt wondering how they were to explain the perpetrator's disappearance into thin air.

Just then the darndest thing happened. The little dog jumped out of the truck and ran straight toward us, panting away and wagging his pathetic little tail. He seemed to have decided he would make friends with us. Of course we did nothing to discourage this behavior since it gave us the perfect opportunity to recover the valuable necklace. Alas, before the poor excuse for a canine could get half way across the parking lot he was intercepted by a human. The man was decked out in full western regalia, from the cowboy boots and plaid shirt right down to the bolo tie and blue jeans.

"Hey little feller," said the human in an appropriately condescending tone of voice. He proceeded to pick up the little mutt and carry him into the trading post, stopping just long enough to make his official statement to the authorities regarding the identity of the car thief, which was essentially, "I didn't see nobody."

10) The Trading Post

After a brief discussion we decided that Princess, Soldier and I would infiltrate the trading post in order to recover the necklace while Gramps would keep an eye on Roscoe and Muffin, who were already busy climbing trees in the nearby woods. A trash can and a drainpipe provided an easy route to a small upper window conveniently left ajar, presumably for ventilation. I volunteered to go first. We were in luck, as directly inside there stood a set of tall shelves for displaying merchandise. Princess and Soldier climbed up and joined me. A quick survey of the place from our lofty perch revealed the establishment to be packed with all sorts of merchandise. Everything from canned goods to Navajo blankets to wood carvings to auto parts seemed to find a home here. A smell vaguely suggestive of leather goods permeated the air. There was a pop machine next to the main entrance, one of those old ones where you lift up the lid and fish the bottle out after depositing the correct change. There appeared to be only two customers in the place, an elderly couple that seemed to think everything was horribly overpriced. The man in the western wear turned out to be the proprietor of the establishment. He stood behind a glass display case cradling the little dog in his left arm. Setting the mutt down on the display case, he proceeded to remove the ruby necklace and clothing. He opened the display case with a key and gently arranged the necklace between a squash blossom and a pearl necklace. Finally he locked the case and stuffed the keys in his pants pocket.

"I wonder if this guy is a cat person," whispered Soldier.

"Only one way to tell," I replied.

"Let me give it a try," said Princess as she looked around for the best route down off of our hiding place. She was just about to leap onto the glass display case when the little dog began to bark at us. The barking was astonishingly loud, considering the diminutive size of the source.

"Cats!" exclaimed the man. "What are a bunch of cats doing in here?" He angrily picked up a broom and lifted it like a baseball batter about to take a swat at one right over home plate. Definitely not a cat person.

"This way!" whispered Soldier. He made for the back of the room, jumping from one shelving unit to another. In the corner stood a heavy-looking dark wood display case with locking glass doors protecting various items of glassware and pottery. The case was situated at a forty-five degree angle to the walls, leaving a triangular area behind that was out of reach of the human and the dog. Soldier jumped down there with Princess and me following right on his heels.

"That was close," said Princess.

"Yeah, what now?" I replied.

"Might as well see what's in here," said Soldier. Sure enough there was a door right there in the corner. It was narrow and had a dusty look about it, like it hadn't been in use for a very long time. Either the door had been left slightly ajar or the latch was broken, because it opened right up when Soldier stood up on his hind legs and gave it a good shove with his paws. There was a small landing and then a stairway leading down into a dimly lit basement. We descended the stairs to find a room full of dusty stacks of boxes, bundles of old newspapers, unknown items covered by tarpaulins, and a few pieces of broken down furniture. In the midst of all this refuse sat a contraption, for lack of a better word, the likes of which I had never seen before.

"You're just in time." The voice belonged to a cat, a tabby and a portly one at that. She sat with her paws on a control panel of sorts, complete with lights and knobs and a great big switch that was attached to said contraption. The contraption itself was made up of numerous portable electronic devices that had been glued, wired, soldered, screwed and otherwise attached to one another. There were cell phones and pagers, radios and remotes, garage door openers and music players. The result was roughly cube shaped with an opening in the front, the interior plenty large enough for one fat cat.

"In time for what?" asked Soldier. The tabby turned toward us and squinted a bit.

"You're not my assistant. What happened to my assistant? I can never depend on that silly kitty."

"I don't know," I ventured. "We just came down here to get away from the man with the broom."

"Oh, him," she chuckled. "Don't worry about him. He's all bark and no bite. Typical dog person. But where are my manners? I'm Tabitha." Once we had made introductions, Princess asked the obvious.

"What is that thing?"

"Why, it's my invention. Behold the world's one and only time machine!" I looked at the contraption and then at Soldier. Soldier looked at me and then looked at Princess. I looked at Princess and Princess looked at me. None of us knew what to say.

"It's not all that complicated, time travel," said Tabitha. "All you need is a strong magnetic field to create a bubble, for lack of a better word, in the time-space continuum. Then you just point in the direction, forward or backward in time that is, you want to go!"

"And to where, I mean to when, do you want to go?"

"Come over here, I'll explain." Tabitha stepped around to one side of the contraption where a large book lay open on the floor. "See here in chapter six, verses fourteen through nineteen. A long long time ago there was a great flood that wiped out everybody and everything except, that is, for one fellow who had the good sense to build himself a great big boat. He and his family got on board and to make sure they'd have a handy supply of meat and eggs and milk, they brought along some cows and chickens and pigs and so on. And of course he brought some cats along for the ride in order to keep the mice at bay. Sadly he got carried away, and along with the useful animals he loaded up two each of the useless ones as well."

"Such as dogs," offered Soldier.

"Such as dogs. So I'll go back to the point in time when the flood waters were about to rise. If the dogs are busy chasing me..."

"They'll miss the boat!" said Princess.

"Brilliant!" I couldn't help but say. The tabby, seeming mighty pleased with herself, fiddled with a few knobs and punched a few buttons on the control panel, then crept into the time machine.

"If one of you would be so kind as to pull the lever."

Princess did the honors, but instead of Tabitha vanishing into the past all that happened was the contraption began to emit a humming sound.

"No worries," said Tabitha, "it just takes a minute or two for the magnetic field to form."

I couldn't tell you whether or not a magnetic field formed, but there were definitely sparks, followed by smoke and flames.

"Oh no, not again!" shouted the tabby. Before you could say *tuna casserole* she was flying up a second stairway in the back of the basement, then out a back door into the woods. The fire spread quickly, what with all the newspapers and broken down furniture providing plenty of fuel. Soldier, Princess and I were quick to follow the mad scientist up the stairs and out the door.

It was late when Princess and I got home. We made a beeline for the cat food.

"There you are! Where have you two been?" said Mary Ann as she gently scratched between my ears. Neither of us, of course, made any reply but kept right on eating. Afterwards we curled up in the den where Ben and Betty were watching the eleven o'clock news on the television.

"Police are searching for the car thief, who seemed to vanish into thin air after crashing into the side of the *Route Fifty-Eight Trading Post*, apparently triggering the fire that burned the establishment to the ground, resulting in a total loss of the building and its contents. Fortunately everyone inside the trading post at the time, including this little dog, escaped with no injuries," said the impeccably groomed news anchorman on the television screen as a photo of the little mutt appeared over his shoulder. The expression on his face conveyed the utmost seriousness. "Our Kelly Wackford caught up with the owner of the car that was stolen."

On the screen appeared an impeccably groomed woman holding a microphone. Next to her stood none other than Aunt Martha, appearing quite ill at ease. "Roger, I'm standing in front of the residence where this afternoon Martha Kowalski had her brand new car stolen right out from under her nose." Turning to Aunt Martha with the air of a funeral director, she asked, "Martha Kowalski, how did it happen?"

"Well, I don't really know. I just went into the house for a moment to tell my sister Betty, that's Betty Bennett, Ben's wife, that I had bought a new car."

"And then, Martha Kowalski, what happened next?"

"Well, I came back outside and the car was gone."

"She came back outside and the car was gone." The woman with the microphone turned to look into the camera and then paused for effect. "Law enforcement officials remind motorists to not leave their keys in the car and never leave the car unattended with the engine running. Back to you Roger."

"Well," said Betty, "Martha always wanted to be on TV. How nice."

11) The Siblings

Princess and I were trying to figure out how to get money to send Mary Ann to rocket science school, now that the valuable ruby necklace was presumably burnt to a crisp. Our brainstorming session wasn't really getting anywhere. Princess said out of the blue, "Do you ever wonder about our brothers and sisters?" The Bennetts had gone to bed and we were relaxing on the cool grass in the back yard. "There were seven or eight of us in the litter, weren't there?"

"Eight as I recall, including you and me."

"Do you have any idea where they ended up?"

"Well," I said, "I imagine one or two of them stayed at the house where we were born. That's clear across town though, and the others could be anywhere."

"Why don't we find out if any of them are still here in town? We could ride the bus over there. It's worth a try."

"How would we go about finding the house? I don't remember much of anything about the old neighborhood. It was a long time ago, and we were just kittens."

"If we can get to the old neighborhood, I'm sure I could find the house."

"Really?" I wiggled my whiskers at her. "What makes you so sure?"

"Because I remember that house. It was different from any of the others. The guy who built it was some sort of an architect. He put in all those long skinny floor-to-ceiling windows and there was no attic, just a flat roof. Don't you remember?"

"Now that you mention it, that was a goofy-looking house. Let's go. I'll bet we can find it!"

Next day we moseyed over to Soldier's house where we found him napping in the grass under a shade tree. We quietly made ourselves comfortable and waited for him to wake up. After all, we weren't in any particular hurry.

Eventually Soldier woke up, and with a yawn said, "How long have you two been here?"

"Not long," I replied.

"Something on your mind?"

"Well, we've been thinking of visiting the other cats from our litter. If we can find them, that is."

"We think one or two of them stayed at the house where we were born," said Princess.

"Of course," I added, "we don't know exactly where the house is, only that it's way over on the other side of town. We were hoping you could get on that internet thingy and help us find the place."

"Sounds iffy, but I'll be glad to help. What do you remember about the house and the neighborhood? Any landmarks that might help us narrow it down? Do you remember the names of any of the streets?"

"I'm afraid not," I admitted. "We were just a few days old when they took us away."

"I do remember distinctly what the house looked like," said Princess earnestly. "It's an odd-looking house, nothing like the others around it." She proceeded to describe the dwelling in detail.

"You're in luck," said Soldier, his ears twitching. "Come on." We followed him through the window with the broken latch and onto his human's computer desk. Soldier punched some letters and numbers on the keyboard, the result of which was the appearance of a bunch of lines, some straight and some curvy, on the screen.

"What's that," asked Princess, "modern art?" She was tilting her furry little head back and forth in an attempt to make sense of it all.

"It's a map of our town, silly," snorted Soldier. "Now all we have to do is look up and down the streets on the far side of town until we find the house."

"But how?" I asked. "This just shows us the streets."

"Watch this," he replied with a grin. Then he pawed at and wiggled that plastic thing that the humans insist on calling a mouse. "This is something I discovered just the other day." He clicked the plastic thing and on the screen appeared a photograph of four houses, side by side. "Now all we have to do is check all of the streets until we find that goofy house of yours. Then we'll find a bus route that takes us there."

"Wow," said Princess, "what'll they think of next?"

Soldier wiggled and punched and clicked away. The computer screen displayed a succession of houses side by side. All of the houses were pretty much the same and not unlike the ones in my neighborhood.

"There it is," exclaimed Princess. One of the houses appeared just as Princess had described it. Soldier worked his magic with the computer and found us a bus route to the other side of town that would get us within shouting distance of the house.

"You'll have to transfer downtown," he said, pawing the center of the map that appeared on the screen. There were numerous zig-zaggy lines of varying colors that mostly converged in the center of the map. Princess and I exchanged looks that said we had no confidence in our ability to pull this off.

"Do you want me to go with you?"

"That would be great," said Princess and I simultaneously. Our heads were nodding and our ears were twitching.

We hopped onto good ol' Route Ten and rode past the Pinewood Mall all the way to downtown. Princess and I had never been downtown before, but Soldier was quite familiar with the area. Store fronts lined the main street, humans strolling past on the wide sidewalks. It was quieter than I had expected as several of the stores were closed down and boarded up.

"That one used to be the drug store until they closed it down and opened a new one in the Pinewood Mall," said Soldier as we passed one of the empty stores.

"But the drug store in the Pinewood Mall closed down," said Princess.

"Did it? Probably moved to the new mall."

"What is it with these humans?" I said to no one in particular. "They can never leave well enough alone."

"Ooooh, that looks like fun," squealed Princess. I had no need to ask what she was talking about, since right in front of us was something the likes of which I had never seen before. Women were coming and going in and out of a dress shop through a contraption that consisted of several glass panels that went around and around.

"What in the world is that thing?" I asked.

"Haven't you ever seen a revolving door?" replied Soldier. "Some of the older stores downtown have 'em. Princess, maybe that's not such a good idea..." It was too late. My sister had jumped inside of the thing and was going around and around. We could hear a meow each time she went by.

"Wait until it stops, Princess, and we'll get you out of there!" I shouted, wondering why there were so many women coming and going. No sooner had I realized my breach of cat etiquette (talking out loud around humans) that I noticed the women kept coming and going as if they hadn't heard anything at all. Then I saw the big signs in the windows of the store advertising a big sale. "This could take a while."

Soldier looked at me and said, "I'm going in," then darted over to the revolving door contraption and jumped into the compartment with Princess. Women, and the occasional man, kept on coming and going so Princess and Soldier kept on going 'round and 'round.

At last I heard a human woman's voice shrieking, "Stop! Everyone stop! There's cats in the door!" Immediately the thing stopped, leaving Princess and Soldier trapped inside until the owner of the voice reached the door and revolved it enough so that the compartment containing the cats opened into the store. She was a neatly attired lady wearing a name tag that identified her as the manager of the store. Fortunately she was a cat person. She picked up Princess with one hand and Soldier with the other and carried them over to a nearby bench.

"Nice kitties. You're safe now." I could see and hear everything because by now I was parked in front of the revolving door contraption. The human directed a younger woman to fetch a nice big bowl of fresh milk. I was feeling left out and let my disappointment be known with a loud sustained meow. I was promptly allowed into the store and did my part to dispose of the cow juice.

It took a few minutes of focused purring to get the nice human lady to let us out of the dress shop. Princess and I followed Soldier towards the bus stop where we would hitch a ride to our destination.

"Mmmm, coffee!" said Princess.

"Yes, what a pleasant aroma," I replied with a sniff. Cats never drink the stuff, but we love the smell. "And where there's coffee..."

"There's pastries!"

The coffee smell was coming from a small coffee shop just down the street from our revolving door adventure. We sneaked into the place, which wasn't at all difficult because the door was one of the sliding-glass variety and had been left in the wide open position, the weather being pleasant that day. The three of us took up residence under a pair of tables that had been pushed together so as to accommodate a gathering of half a dozen humans. While waiting for a chance to snatch some sweet morsels we eavesdropped on the conversation.

"...so I hope you're all with me on this," said a man wearing brown wing tips. "I can't overstate the importance of us offering a salary and benefit package that's competitive with nearby towns of our population classification."

"Well, I think we are all in agreement," said a woman in blue leather pumps, "but I don't know how we're supposed to explain a quintupling of the mayor's salary to the public."

"And some of us are up for re-election this year," added a man in black loafers.

"That's right," said a woman in really expensive athletic shoes, "we have to consider that."

"Just remember to point out that the reasons for the increase are twofold," replied Brown Wing Tips. "First and foremost, over the years the position has evolved from a part-time job to one that requires a full-time commitment. Second, the salary has been frozen for the last fifteen years. Do you know how much the cost of living has increased in that time?"

The sundry mumbles and clearing of throats emanating from the humans (Blue Leather Pumps, Really Expensive Athletic Shoes, and Black Loafers sharing the tables with Cowboy Boots and Sandals) led me to believe that there was some confusion as to whether or not the question was meant to be rhetorical.

"Sixty-eight percent!" exclaimed Brown Wing Tips. So the question was not meant to be rhetorical.

"That much?" queried Sandals sheepishly.

"Well, that's good to know," mumbled Cowboy Boots.

Of course this talk was music to my ears. If Ben Bennett could get himself elected mayor, he would surely be able to afford to send Mary Ann to rocket science school.

We waited around for a while but didn't find a single scrap of pastry. Apparently every member of the city council was on a diet and resolved to limit coffee breaks to just coffee. Soldier soon found the right bus stop and we hopped onto the Route Forty-Four with no trouble. The ride seemed to go by quickly, with Princess and me looking out the window at scenery that was new to us. I hardly need to mention that the humans paid us no mind, their eyes glued to the screens of their electronic devices. One man slept the whole time we were on the bus, clutching his smart phone with both hands as if it were a tiny pillow. Fortunately he was not the driver.

Thanks to Soldier's research on the computer interwebs thingamajig, we were able to find the house with no trouble at all. It looked just like in the picture except for several rolled-up newspapers littering the lawn, which had turned a shade of brownish-green. A cat occupied one of the two metal chairs on a porch off to the right of the front door. We politely sat down on the sidewalk until he let out a friendly meow. I padded up the front walk followed by Princess and then Soldier. The cat hopped off his chair and looked at me closely for a moment.

"Do I know you?"

"I'm Clarence, and this is Princess, and Soldier over here. I believe you're from the same litter as Princess and I."

"Well how about that! I knew you looked familiar, by golly, how long has it been? Oh, but where are my manners? My name is Bob The Cat. Delighted to see you!"

"Your name is *Bob The Cat*, not just *Bob?*" asked Soldier.

"Yeah, my humans let their five-year-old name me. What can you do?"

"There don't seem to be any humans around here," I said, surveying the thirsty lawn and rolled-up newspapers.

"You're right about that," sighed Bob The Cat. "The human who lives here started growing stuff that humans aren't supposed to grow. Catnip for humans, if you catch my drift."

"Say no more."

"Anyway, the wife and kids split a year ago and the guy is currently residing in the barbed-wire hotel."

"Cool!" said Princess with enthusiasm, "you've got the place to yourself, Bob. Excuse me, *Bob The Cat*."

"Well, yeah, it's great and all, but there's no one around to feed me. I've taken to begging at neighbors' kitchen doors, and this is pretty much a dog lovers' neighborhood so it ain't easy."

"Not to worry," I said, looking at Princess and Soldier, "what do you say we take a ride and get this fellow a decent meal?"

"You mean the fish and chips shop?" Princess was licking her lips.

"Sure, why not?"

"The last time we were there it was slim pickin's."

"Yeah, but that's just because they'd cleaned up the joint for the health inspector. By now things should be back to normal."

We trotted down to the bus stop and gave Bob The Cat a lesson on the use of public transportation. After changing buses downtown, carefully avoiding the vicinity of any revolving doors, we arrived at the Pinewood Mall. We were relieved to find that the usual attendant was back at the fish and chips shop, calmly enjoying his cancer stick outside the rear door.

"Come on, Bob The Cat," I said, "it's dinner time!" I slipped inside the fish and chips shop, the door of course having been propped open, followed by Bob The Cat, then Princess and Soldier. The *thump thump thump* of the jukebox filled the air and little bits of light flitted across the ceiling. The teenage girl was back to sitting on the overturned five-gallon drum, phone glued to her ear. The kitchen was messier than ever with bits of fish and fries strewn about on the floor. Apparently once the health inspector had come and gone, cleanliness had reverted back to its usual priority, that being the lowest.

"Wow!" exclaimed Bob The Cat. "Like... wow!"

"Be my guest," said Princess. Bob The Cat didn't wait to be asked twice and began to scarf down fish fragments like there was no tomorrow. After we had all had a good meal, and let me tell you there was plenty to go around, we hopped up onto the counter to watch the disco dancers. None of the humans seemed to notice us, the fish and chips man still outside smoking, the teenage girl still on the phone, and the disco dancers caught up in the music and the light show.

"Hey, look. Kittens!" said Bob The Cat.

"Friends of ours," said Soldier. "That's Roscoe, and that's Muffin." The kittens were playing a game, taking turns making a mad dash from one end of the dance floor to the other, the object being to see who could cross the most times without getting stepped on, tripped over or otherwise interfered with. We watched for a while, the dexterity being demonstrated by the kittens indicating that we were in for a lengthy performance. Once we'd had enough entertainment we went outside and found a shady spot on a strip of lawn.

12) The TV Station

Autumn arrived, and with it the leaves turned from green to red and gold. A chilly night gave way to a pleasantly sunny Monday, the day before Election Day. Princess and Soldier were off somewhere hunting for mice. Bob The Cat had no desire to return to his house across town and had been adopted by the Bennetts. We decided to go down to the mall and, accompanied by Roscoe and Muffin, we moseyed down to the bus stop where we sat under the bench to wait for Route Ten. By now we had a pretty good idea as to when the bus was likely to stop there to let someone off, humans being creatures of habit. Sure enough the big vehicle came roaring up the street and wheezed to a halt. The same guy who got off the bus there every weekday at eleven-thirty soon appeared on the threshold of the back door. As he stepped onto the sidewalk, we climbed up the steps and made ourselves comfortable on an empty seat.

After an uneventful ride to the Pinewood Mall, we slipped into the fish and chips shop for a snack. It was too early for us to be entertained by the dancing at the disco food court, so Bob The Cat and I sauntered over to the coffee shop for some eavesdropping while Roscoe and Muffin wandered off to explore. A spot under a booth allowed us to hear everything said by two humans, a male and a female, seated at a table in the back corner.

"I don't know what else I can do," said the man, who wore a business suit. I recognized him as Ben's opponent.

"I've denied any responsibility for the bogus press release, but nobody believes me."

"Look," said the woman, who was neatly attired in a sky blue mid-length skirt and white blouse, "I've got the latest poll numbers and as it stands you don't have a chance."

"So that's it? We're done?"

"Not necessarily. Do you watch football?"

"Of course I do."

"So you're familiar with the term *Hail Mary pass*?"

"Sure. What do you have in mind?"

The woman went on to explain her desperation plan. The candidate would change his tune and take responsibility for the ridiculous ideas contained in the press release. He would go on live television that evening, somberly declaring that he has learned his lesson and humbly asking the voters for forgiveness.

"But I'll be admitting that I lied about it before!" he protested.

"So what? The voters know that all politicians lie through their teeth. Give 'em a heartfelt apology, though, and they eat it up like a piece of chocolate cake."

"I suppose it's worth a try," said the politician in a voice thoroughly lacking in enthusiasm, "I mean, what have I got to lose?"

"That's the spirit!" The woman in the blue dress went on to inform the candidate that she had already made arrangements for him to appear on the town's television station at seven o'clock sharp.

Well, we weren't about to take a chance that Ben's lead in the polls would stand up to this kind of shenanigans. This telecast would not go on the air, not if Bob The Cat I had anything to say about it. We were determined to march right down to that TV station and pull the plug on the transmitter. Of course we would have to figure out where exactly the TV station was, what the heck a transmitter looked like, and how exactly to unplug it. I decided to recruit Roscoe and Muffin to accompany us and create a diversion so we would have plenty of time to find and disable the transmitter. Too bad Soldier wasn't around. We could have used his help finding the TV station with that internet thing. Oh well, we would just have to find another way.

"Those TV news people," said Bob The Cat thoughtfully, "there's a pretty good chance we would find one or more of them downtown on any given day. Don't ya think?"

"Yes," I replied, "you're probably right."

"So we ride the bus downtown and when we find one or two of them we, what do you call it, tag along. Hopefully right back to the station."

For lack of any better ideas we rounded up the kittens and pawed it over to the bus stop. After an uneventful ride downtown we took to wandering about in search of TV news people. The streets were devoid of any sort of van or vehicle sporting TV station logos. Just when we were about to start racking our little cat brains for a Plan B, Roscoe spotted a couple of humans in blue blazers. These would likely be TV news people because TV news people just love to wear those blue blazers. The two were walking briskly side by side down the sidewalk, the one on the left nervously jingling the set of keys in his right hand. They soon approached a nondescript white two-door car. While it was lacking in any sort of logos, somehow it looked like the kind of car a couple of TV news people would tool around town in.

"But how can we be sure they're actually TV news people?" queried Bob The Cat, quite reasonably.

"Shhh... listen," I whispered.

"Just one hour until show time," said the human with the car keys. "We're in good shape." Sounded like a TV news person to me.

"Positions!" I said, trying desperately to inject authority into my voice. You will recall, a tag-along only works with one cat per car door. We had arranged for Roscoe and Muffin to ride "piggyback" on Bob The Cat and I in order for all of us to board at once. Brilliant, if I do say so myself. It was close, but we made it without any damage to our tails. The blazers didn't say much on the drive to the TV station, and what little they said sounded like a bunch of gobbledygook to me. I had no idea TV stuff was so technical.

After a ride that lasted maybe fifteen or twenty minutes, we came to what I assumed was our destination. The car had come to a stop and the driver's side window was quickly rolled down. Some very serious sounding person outside the car asked the blazer people for identification, a request that was promptly answered with the display of a couple of laminated documents. It sure seemed like overkill in the security department, you know, for just a TV station. When the car came to a halt and the doors flew open, we were ready to go in "piggyback" position. After leaping out the doors for our little rendezvous under the car, we managed to follow the two humans in blazers into a windowless building that supported a forest of antennae on its flat roof. At the end of a brief corridor we emerged into a large room with a high ceiling. Several rows of humans sat in front of television monitors like birds perched on telephone wires. There was a huge screen on the opposite wall on which we could see a rocket on a launching pad, an ever-changing digital display in the foreground indicating a few minutes and seconds until what a viewer could only assume would be liftoff.

"Surely the candidate will be going on as soon as this science fiction movie is over with," whispered Bob The Cat.

"No doubt," I replied. "Okay kitties, you know what to do!" With that Roscoe and Muffin jumped onto a couple of consoles and began to play with the knobs and buttons and switches as if they were cat toys.

"Code red!" shouted someone. "Malfunction! Code red!" In the ensuing chaos Bob The Cat and I managed to make our way into an adjoining room, smaller and with a lower ceiling than the other, and full of electronic equipment, the metal boxes adorned with all kinds of blinking lights. Looked like transmitters to me. Slithering behind the boxes, Bob The Cat and I systematically clawed at the power cords until we had unplugged them all. Humans were running this way and that, shouting all sorts of official-sounding things, but quite oblivious to the presence of two full grown and two miniature cats. We met up with Roscoe and Muffin near the entrance and didn't have to wait long until a couple of humans went bursting through the door, leaving it wide open and making our escape as easy as pie.

We were feeling mighty pleased with ourselves for about ten seconds. And then we saw the sign at the entrance to what we now knew was not the television station:

United States Air Force
Pinewood Missile Launching Facility
Authorized Personnel Only

"Ooops!" was all I could manage to say. Bob The Cat was speechless but Roscoe and Muffin were rolling around on the ground in fits of laughter as if was the funniest thing they'd ever seen. So there we were way out on the outskirts of town where the buses don't run with the clock surely approaching seven o'clock. What the actual time was we couldn't say, cats not being in the habit of carrying timepieces.

"I wonder if we could somehow get a ride back into town," said Bob The Cat.

"I doubt it," I replied, noting that the only vehicles that were going anywhere were all headed towards the facility, most of them with angrily flashing red lights and screaming sirens. "Let's climb that hill over there and have a look around. It beats sitting around here, don't you think?" The others agreed and we climbed up the hill at a brisk pace.

Surveying the town from the summit, I spotted a building with the TV station logo lit up in the deepening dusk. We hightailed it down the other side of the hill and soon arrived at the front door of the station. There weren't any humans coming or going to open the door so we circled around the building and fortunately found a window that had been left wide open. The four of us were soon inside traipsing up and down hallways in search of the studio from which the candidate's speech would originate.

"Do you hear that?" said Roscoe, his little ears twitching.

"Yeah, it's coming from in there," said Muffin, nodding towards a door that had been left cracked open just a bit. We silently crept up to the opening and listened.

"What do you mean pre-empted?" The voice sounded furious. "You can't pre-empt us. We have to go on this evening. Tomorrow's Election Day!" I peeked inside and recognized the speaker as the politician's lackey that I had seen at the mall.

"I'm sorry," said a woman who was standing directly opposite the lackey. She wore a dark green pantsuit, her brown hair neatly tied back in a bun, "but the sabotage at the missile facility is a breaking news story, and a big one at that. You've got to understand, we have to cover it live."

"But I have a contract that says my candidate goes on at seven o'clock sharp." He reached into his suit coat pocket and whipped out some paperwork. His facial expression was equal parts triumph and hostility.

s

"Well sir, if you'll refer to paragraph nine, subparagraph C you'll see that in the event of a breaking news story the station reserves the right to pre-empt any and all programming until such time as the breaking news story is no longer..."

At this point the lackey shouted something unintelligible and stormed off somewhere. It seemed that our work here was done. Now to see if we could find a ride home.

We tried a hallway that we hadn't yet explored, ending up in the main lobby at the front of the building. It was deserted and the lights dimmed, but a television set mounted on the wall was on, tuned of course to the live coverage of the sabotage of the missile facility. We made ourselves comfortable on the faux leather sofas that were conveniently arranged so as to have a good view of the TV. On the screen was a man in a military uniform with lots of badges and things stuck to it, which I took to mean that he was the highest-ranking guy around. He was responding to some leading questions from a disembodied interviewer's voice with assurances that the situation was under control and there was no danger to the public and everything was going to be just fine. The interviewer then appeared on the screen. I recognized her as the same woman who had interviewed Aunt Martha the day we borrowed her car. She said something about the preceding statement seeming incongruous with the frantic activity taking place all around her. Then she just stood there staring at the camera, clearly having run out of things to say. After an awkward several seconds, the news anchor appeared on the screen. He had nothing to add regarding the missile facility crisis, and promised that viewers would not want to miss the live speech by a mayoral candidate that was coming up right after the commercial break. So it promised to be a close election after all.

Our eyeballs were so glued to the TV set that we hadn't noticed a woman in the room. It was the one in the green pantsuit. Fortunately she turned out to be a cat person and soon was feeding us dishes of milk and some leftover tuna fish out of a plastic container that she found in a refrigerator somewhere. After a nice meal and some focused purring, she took us to her car and gave us a ride to the Bennett's house where we all had a nice long nap.

13) The Airport

Election Day arrived and Ben's family, friends and campaign workers were assembled at the Bennett house. The place was packed with people, chilly weather preventing the use of the patio and yard. The mood was tense, Ben's opponent having narrowed the gap in the polls due to a masterfully manipulative speech. A television set had been placed on top of the bar in the den so as to provide as many guests as possible with a view of the election results. Princess, Bob The Cat, and I were parked under the coffee table in the living room where a news crew from a local television station was preparing for a live broadcast. I recognized the interviewer as the anchorperson who appeared on the Bennett's TV set every evening at six. Ben was seated on the sofa with Betty on one side and Mary Ann on the other.

"Come on, kids. Don't you want to be on TV?" shouted Ben.

"I don't think they heard," said Betty. "Mary Ann, would you go round up the boys?"

"Sure, Mom."

"Come on," I whispered, "this is our chance to be on TV!" I hopped onto the sofa and sat down next to Ben. Bob The Cat took his place next to Betty and Princess made herself comfortable on Mary Ann's lap.

"Sorry about that," said Mary Ann to the interviewer. She picked Princess up and was about to deposit her on the floor when the TV lady said, "no, that's okay. Let the cats stay."

"Yeah, I like it," said a man wearing headphones with a little microphone attached. He was peering out from behind the camera. "The cats are a nice touch."

Max and Joey joined in, sitting on the floor in front of the others. Just for fun I turned my posterior toward the camera and began to wave my tail back and forth. Max picked me up and sat me down facing the camera.

"Behave yourself, Clarence."

"Okay, lights!" came a voice from behind the camera. Suddenly the room was flooded with light, the brightest light I'd ever seen. Except perhaps for the sun, but I'm not in the habit of staring at the sun and these two white hot circles were pointed right in our faces. Cats, as you might have guessed, don't care for this sort of thing one bit. Princess, Bob The Cat, and I simultaneously leaped onto the coffee table and then onto the floor, running at full speed until we were safely under an end table in the den.

"So much for that idea," I could hear the camera man say as we flew by.

When the election returns came in it was close, but Ben lost the election. Personally I suspect voter fraud, but I can't prove it. The next day Princess, Soldier and I took Bob The Cat over to meet Gramps, who gave him a tour of the big old house. It was something he enjoyed very much, having never seen the insides of a big old house.

"Don't worry, we've got the place to ourselves," said Gramps as we wandered the hallways and rooms. "My human is at the golf course all day as usual. So Clarence, have you told Bob The Cat about focused purring yet?"

"He's seen me do it," I replied. "That's how we got a ride home from the TV station."

"Would you like to learn it?"

"Would I? Of course I would," replied Bob The Cat.

"Come on down to the basement," said Gramps.

After Gramps had given Bob The Cat his focused purring lesson, we lounged around making idle chat. We eventually got around to the subject of the whereabouts of the other five kittens in our litter. According to Bob The Cat, they were all adopted by a family who lived in a town some distance to the north of us.

"Too bad we can't tag-along on an airplane," sighed Princess. "It would be so nice to see them again."

"Who says we can't?" Soldier had a mischievous look in his eyes. "As far as I know, it's never been done. But that doesn't mean it can't be done!"

Having made up our minds to catch a ride on an airplane, the first order of business was to get to the airport. We would need to make a stop at Soldier's house so he could get on that computer thing and figure out how we could get there and find the right plane.

"Gramps, would you like to come with us?"

"No thanks," replied the old cat with a yawn, "I think I'll take a nap. I will, however, give you one piece of advice. Don't try to take the whole gang along with you, not on the first attempt. Just two of you should go. Something tells me it won't be anything like riding the bus."

Joined by Roscoe and Muffin, we entered Soldier's house in the usual way through the window with the broken latch and gathered around the computer monitor. Our host started pounding on the keyboard and clicking that thing that, I'm sorry but I just don't get it, humans insist upon calling a *mouse*. Soldier gave Roscoe and Muffin something to play with so that they wouldn't try to eat the so-called mouse. It was one of those cheesy rubber cat toys that humans often buy for us.

"Okay," said Soldier, "You're going to take Amalgamated Air Flight Three Sixty-Four departing from Gate Five at 10:17am. However, I'm afraid the city bus system doesn't have a route that goes to the airport. Route Forty-Four comes the closest, but it's another half a mile and some pretty treacherous street crossings to get to the terminal."

"I don't like the sound of that," said Princess.

"Well," I said, "there's got to be another way. What about a tag-along?"

"That could work," replied Soldier, turning to face Bob The Cat and me, "but only two of us could go. And you would have to find a car that's going to the airport."

"Didn't your friend Gramps say that we should try it with only two cats?" asked Bob The Cat, directing the question at me. Soldier agreed that only two cats should make the first attempt at catching a plane. Then he started warning us about the perils of the airport.

"You don't just waltz in there and take your seat on the airplane, oh no, you've got to get past *Security!*

"Security?" queried Princess. "Like the security guards at the mall?"

"Sort of, except these are bigger and meaner. And there are lots more of them."

"I don't like the sound of that at all," said Princess. "I volunteer to stay home." And thus it was decided that Bob The Cat and I would be the ones to attempt the first known tag-along on an airplane.

"Hmmmm, this might work," said Soldier. He was scrolling through some sort of a list on the computer screen, then clicked the so-called mouse.

"What's that?"

"I searched on *airport transportation* to see what came up, just in case there's something I hadn't thought of. Look here, most of the hotels operate these shuttle buses to take their guests to and from the airport. Now they're smaller buses, more the size of a van like the ones humans use to go camping. You should be able to slip aboard one of them."

Soldier then punched and clicked some more and the screen displayed a list of hotels in or near downtown that included airport transportation among their amenities. We had our choice of the *Royal Lion Inn,* the *Lavish Lodge,* the *High Life Hotel,* or the *Merry Mansion.* Although it was tempting to choose the one with a cat in the name, we settled on the Merry Mansion, it being the one closest to the bus stop.

Bob The Cat and I caught the earliest bus the next morning so as to give us plenty of time to make it to the airport and board our flight. When we arrived downtown, a bright green little bus was parked in front of the hotel. On the side was painted *Merry Mansion, you'll check out with a smile on your face.* The door was wide open, so we hopped in and curled up under the bench in the middle. Soon humans began boarding, glumly marching in and plopping down on the seats as if they wished they were still in bed.

I was expecting the van to start moving, but it sat still for what seemed like an awfully long time. I began to doze and was awakened by that unique sound, somewhere between a grind and a squeak, which announced an internal combustion engine's refusal to start. The humans on board began to mumble and grumble, each one declaring that he or she absolutely positively must not miss their flight because they had places to go, things to do, and people (*important* people) to see! They were far from merry, and if I could have seen their faces I doubt I would have seen a smile among them. Hadn't they read the side of the van? The driver of the vehicle, after somewhat unconvincingly suggesting that the delay would be brief, hurried into the hotel and returned a few minutes later. He was accompanied by a man in coveralls who was carrying what appeared to be a large brick.

"Just replacing the battery," said one of the passengers. "Shouldn't take long." Fortunately he wasn't wrong and shortly we were on our way. All the way to the airport the humans kept talking about how they were barely going to be in time to catch their flight, and what a shame it would be if they missed it because of all the places they had to go, the things they needed to do, and most of all, the people (*important* people) they needed to see.

The instant the van stopped at the airport terminal the doors flew open and humans popped out like biscuit dough from one of those cardboard cylinders when it's whacked against the kitchen counter. They all grabbed their luggage and sprinted into the terminal building, still chattering about the places they had to... well, you get the idea. Bob The Cat and I followed and hid behind one of two planters that each held a tall skinny evergreen tree, one on either side of the main entrance. Here we took a moment to assess the situation and plan our next move. Humans were coming and going through some big glass doors that formed the entrance to the terminal building. They were those doors that open automatically when one or more humans approach but have a habit of ignoring cats. There were so many people dashing in and out with their various pieces of luggage that the door seldom closed for more than a second or two.

"Man alive, that looks scary," said Bob The Cat.

"Yeah," I replied, "this could be tricky." We both poked our heads out from behind the planter and scanned our surroundings. "Are you thinking what I'm thinking?" We were looking at a wooded area off to one side of the terminal building. With any luck we could circle around through there and reach the runway unseen, thereby avoiding the whole airport terminal and security mess.

14) The Airliner

"This is nice," I said as we strolled across the floor of leaves and pine needles. "It's cool and shady in here."

"Hey, look!" exclaimed Bob The Cat, "a wild rabbit."

"I beg your pardon, sir. Just because I live in the woods and not in a cage does not mean I am wild."

"Wow, you can talk."

"Of course I can talk," replied the rabbit with an indignant air. "What did you think I was, a dumb bunny?"

"Oh no, not at all," said Bob The Cat quickly, "I just never knew rabbits could talk." I shrugged to indicate *neither did I.* "No offense."

"None taken," replied the rabbit with a slight wiggle of his ears. "Allow me to introduce myself. Horace T. Hopp, at your service. You're not from around here, or you would know all about talking rabbits. We've lived here in these woods for years, long before the humans built this dreadful airport."

"I'm Clarence," I said, "from across town. And this is Bob The Cat. He lives down the road a ways."

"Really, you came from clear across town? As in on the other side of downtown?" Mr. Hopp looked incredulous. "You must have been walking for days."

"No, we took the bus."

"The bus! Positively amazing! But where are my manners? Please, step into my humble abode for some refreshments."

"Is your rabbit hole nearby?" I asked. Looking around, all I could see was a dilapidated old dog house that was mostly obscured by the underbrush.

"Rabbit hole!" exclaimed Mr. Hopp with a chuckle. "Oh no, I haven't lived in a hole in a long time. Not since I moved into my house. Come, right this way." Sure enough, the rabbit hopped on over to the doghouse and disappeared inside. Bob The Cat and I still had plenty of time before our flight left and, rabbits generally being perfectly harmless, we decided we might as well take him up on his offer. We crept up to the doghouse and Bob The Cat poked his head in first.

"Whoa..... nice!"

I stuck my head in beside him and agreed with his assessment. The original occupant must have been a large breed, as the place was rather roomy. There were several pillows in various states of repair, none of them matching, strewn around on the floor. One large one in particular had a rabbit-sized indentation in the center. It was situated so as to provide an optimal view of a small television set in the corner. In the other corner, to my utter amazement, was a small stove of the kind humans take with them on camping trips. The stove sat on top of an old metal breadbox, and upon the stove was a tea kettle.

"Make yourselves at home." Our host proceeded to turn a knob on the stove with his teeth. Immediately a flame appeared under the teapot. "Do you take milk in your tea?" We were still standing on the threshold, too astonished to move. "Come in, come in!" We did so, and took our places on the pillows. "Now, do you take milk in your tea?" asked Mr. Hopp impatiently.

"Ummm... yes," I replied.

"Yes, please. I'll take milk," said Bob The Cat politely. "Actually, you can just hold the tea and give me the milk," he added under his breath. We both had to stifle a laugh. The rabbit then grabbed a button on the TV with his teeth and pulled.

"The ballgame should be starting any minute."

"Have you got cable?" asked Soldier as the screen came to life.

"Nope, just the rabbit ears."

We sat with the rabbit and sipped tea, which wasn't half bad, and told him all about riding the bus and our plan to catch a plane and search for our long-lost siblings. Then I explained how we figured we could circumvent security by circling through the woods to the runway.

"Not gonna happen," said the rabbit, shaking his head. "They've got it all fenced off, and they're big fences with barbed wire on the top. Security guards patrol it, too. You're only way is through the terminal."

"I guess we had better get going then," I said. Mr. Hopp must have read the looks on our faces.

"Now don't worry," he said, suddenly sitting up on his hind legs, "getting through security is a piece of cake. If you've got help, that is. Come on, let's do this thing."

Soon two cats and a rabbit were hiding behind a mountain of luggage. Several lines of harried-looking travelers had formed in front of the security screening stations. Each of the humans placed their luggage, purses, packages, shopping bags, wrist watches, cameras, and other sundry items into plastic buckets on conveyor belts.

They then proceeded to empty their pockets of keys, coins, wallets, phones, tissues, lozenges, bus tokens and half-eaten candy bars. I half expected them to disrobe on the spot. Two or three of the big mean security guards stood at each station decked out in navy blue uniforms with shiny badges and photo ID's displayed prominently in plastic attached to thick black lanyards.

"Are you sure about this?" whispered Bob The Cat, leaning back slightly on his hind legs, which I knew meant that he was just about ready to bolt and run.

"Don't worry, I've got this," said Mr. Hopp with a halfway grin. "Let's go!"

The rabbit took off in the direction of the screening station like a bale of cotton shot out of a cannon. Hopping onto a conveyor belt, he swatted the bags, purses, phones and other items into the air and onto the floor. The security guards and travelers stood stunned for a moment and then as if on cue began to run around in circles, jumping up and down shouting at one another. Red lights started blinking on and off, accompanied by regularly repeating buzzing sounds of a semi-deafening intensity. I hardly need to mention that Bob The Cat and I were able to stroll right through the chaos to our gate unobserved in plenty of time to board our flight. We waved our thanks to Mr. Horace T. Hopp as he bounded away toward the main entrance.

"Hmmm, this could be tricky," I said as Bob The Cat and I sat under a bench in the waiting area of Gate Ten. Some humans had formed a line at a counter behind which stood a young redheaded woman dressed in a uniform of the same dark blue as that of the security guards' garb. Something about the cut of the fabric, however, seemed to make her appear friendly while the security guards' uniforms seemed designed for intimidation. She was taking pieces of paper from the human at the front of the line, apparently scribbling something on the papers, and then handing the papers back to the humans. After each of these operations she would chirp, "Have a nice flight, sir," or "Have a nice flight, ma'am," whichever the case may be. Once she hesitated for a moment and simply said, "Have a nice flight." Then the passengers got in line before an entryway to a narrow corridor which I assumed led to the airplane. If I didn't know better, I would have said that the primary purpose of an airport was to ensure that the maximum number of humans would be standing in line for the maximum amount of time.

"Yeah," murmured Bob The Cat, once again appearing ready to abandon ship, "how are we supposed to get in there?"

"I've got it! Watch and learn, my friend. Then follow me." With this I darted over to the boarding line and carefully crouched at the heels of a human whose right hand was clutching his piece of paper while his left hand held a handle that was attached to a suitcase with two little wheels that allowed him to pull the suitcase behind him like a kid with a little red wagon. The suitcase shielded me from view of the other passengers in the line. I had to be cautious and follow right on the human's heels each time the line moved so as to avoid getting run over by the suitcase. I managed to poke my head out enough to sneak a peek just in time to see my companion get in line with a human of his own.

Well, Gramps was right. The plane wasn't anything at all like the bus. Bob The Cat and I scampered down the narrow aisle desperately looking for a hiding place. Every seat on the plane was taken up by one human or another. The seats were so narrow that the humans could barely avoid touching the other humans on either side of them. The rows of seats were crammed in so tight that all but the shortest passengers had their knees stuck right up against the seat in front of them. The spaces under the seats were inexplicably crammed full of all the items that the humans (I thought) had left behind on the little conveyor belts. The cabin of that airplane was downright claustrophobic, and this is coming from a creature who thinks it's loads of fun to crawl into paper bags! We got to the rear of the cabin and managed to hide in a cupboard inside a tiny room that smelled of coffee and pastries.

"Whew, that was rough," I said, exhaling. Bob The Cat just sat there with that expression on his face that a deer has at night when suddenly illuminated by the headlights of an oncoming car. Soon we felt a slight jolt and surmised that the airplane was being moved from the terminal to the runway in anticipation of its takeoff into the wild blue yonder. "Don't worry, buddy, I'm sure the worst is over. We'll be in the air before you can say *great big ball of yarn.*" I could not have been more wrong. We sat there. And sat there. And sat there. It seemed like hours had passed when the feet of what was apparently a young man, clad in the same dark blue as the others, appeared just outside our hiding place. The owner of the feet was engaged in a conversation with someone out of my range of vision.

"It's complimentary coffee and sodas for everyone, you hear?"

"Yeah?"

"Yeah. It looks like we're going to be here for a while."

"I thought they said the weather had cleared up."

"It did, but now they have to fix the hydraulics."

I don't pretend to know what a hydraulics is, but it sure sounded important. So my furry friend and I sat there, no alternative coming to mind. Through all of this we could hear a muffled voice coming over the public address system, cheerfully promising the passengers a minimal delay and a delightful flight to come. Little by little the passengers grew surly. Mumbling turned to complaining. Complaining turned to shouting. The cabin began to take on the atmosphere of a stick of dynamite with the fuse lit. Perhaps pumping everyone full of caffeine was not the best idea. Well, Bob The Cat and I decided we'd had enough and made a break for it. As we sprinted down the aisle, humans started screaming at the top of their lungs.

"Cats on the plane! Cats on the plane!" They threw paper coffee cups at us, not all of them completely empty, and swatted at us with rolled-up in-flight magazines. When we reached the front of the plane it dawned on me that the door was sealed shut. We were trapped inside an airplane full of caffeine-stoked angry humans with no way out. Or so I thought. Bob The Cat, fortunately, had paid more attention than I to the safety instructions given by one of the humans in the dark blue suits.

"Come on, follow me. Quickly!" He darted back down the aisle and I followed because really, what else was I going to do? After passing a dozen or so rows of seats Bob The Cat stopped on a dime and then leaped up onto the lap of the human in the aisle seat. That person, an elderly woman dressed conservatively in a gray dress and jacket, well, she was obviously not a cat person. She let out a shriek that could possibly have been heard from the terminal and then lifted her rolled-up in-flight magazine in anticipation of giving my comrade a good whack. Bob The Cat, however, bounced from her lap onto the lap of the human in the middle seat, then onto the lap of the person in the window seat, and then threw himself against the side of the cabin, which turned out to be the emergency exit. His two front paws grasped a big red lever and a door swung open accompanied by a loud hissing sound. The three humans had each taken a swat at him with their rolled-up in-flight magazines and each had nothing to show for the effort. The hissing sound was caused by the inflating of the emergency exit slide, onto which Bob The Cat disappeared. All of this transpired in a matter of just a few seconds. The humans were momentarily distracted by the inflating slide, allowing me to waltz right across their laps and slide down to safety. Bob The Cat and I ran across the hot tarmac in no particular direction just as fast as our paws would carry us.

15) The Flight

Bob The Cat and I ran across the runway until we left the pavement and felt cool grass beneath our paws. I wasn't aware of the wailing sirens until we had both plopped down on the lawn to catch our breath. Looking back, I could see that several vehicles sporting flashing red lights had converged upon the airplane.

"That was awful," said Bob The Cat. "Let's not ever try that again."

"Agreed." My brother suggested we try boarding one of those buses that goes from town to town, but I nipped that idea right in the bud. No way am I riding in a vehicle with a picture of a *dog* on the side! There had to be another way.

"I guess we should go back and let the others know what happened."

"Might as well," I replied. We started walking and soon came to a hedge, which we slipped through with no trouble. On the other side was a building, much smaller than the airport terminal, around which sat several airplanes. These planes were tiny compared to the one from which we had just made our escape. "How about that. A baby airport."

Of course our curiosity got the best of us and in spite of the vow we had taken not five minutes prior we marched right over to the entrance. The big glass door required a human to push on the handle in order for it to open, so we sat and waited for one to arrive. The baby airport obviously saw nowhere near the level of foot traffic as the grownup airport, so we sat there for a while.

The entryway was devoid of shrubbery, trash cans, and any other potential hiding places so we took our chances sitting there out in the open. After all, what's the worst that could happen? Don't answer that.

Just about the time we were ready to call it a day, a taxicab pulled up and discharged two human passengers. One was a woman, smartly attired in a dark green dress and a blouse with a pretty flower print. I guessed her to be in her fifties. She waited for the driver to remove two suitcases from the trunk of the car, then handed him some paper money and advised him to keep the change. I could see she was a generous tipper from the enthusiastic thanks expressed by the cabbie. I guessed the other human to be her daughter, which was confirmed soon enough.

"Look mom, cats!"

"I see, Emma."

Now, hearing these words will cause varying reactions in cats depending on the tone of voice and body language of the speakers. We were perfectly calm because by their manner it was obvious to us that these two humans were cat people. The two approached and crouched down to pet us, saying things like, "nice kitty," and "what are you doing so far from home, pretty cat?" Then they picked up their suitcases and the daughter held the door open to allow her mother to go inside. Instead of following her, though, she continued to hold the door open. It took a moment, but I realized that there were no other humans around and she was holding the door open for Bob The Cat and me.

The baby airport was so much nicer than the grownup one. There were no crowds, no conveyor belts, and none of those big mean security guards. A few nicely dressed and seemingly very polite humans were sitting on upholstered benches. On the wall to our left was displayed a huge map, presumably of the surrounding area, complete with red circles and lines which no doubt imparted useful information to the humans who flew the airplanes from place to place. Straight ahead was a counter that stood in front of a wall of floor-to-ceiling windows that offered a view of the little airplanes parked outside. Against the wall opposite the gigantic map was the counter of a fast-food establishment, the neon sign that seemed to hover above it appropriately reading *Snack Bar*. The elder woman approached the young man who stood behind the counter and said, "A carton of milk and two bowls, please." Since humans are generally not in the habit of drinking their milk out of bowls, I surmised that the treat was for us. Sure enough, she walked over to us and poured us each a bowl of milk.

"It will be about fifteen minutes before the plane is ready for us to board," said the daughter, having just returned from the counter over by the windows. She sat down next to her mother on one of the benches. From the ensuing conversation, Bob The Cat and I discovered that their destination was to be the same city where we were going to look for our siblings. As soon as we had finished our milk, each of us took our place on a lap and took to purring. It didn't take but two minutes for the women to decide on a last-minute addition of two cats to their passenger list.

"We're all set, Mrs. Morland, Miss Morland," said a man wearing a light blue shirt and khaki slacks. He was holding a glass door open. The elder Morland picked me up and held me with her right arm while lifting her suitcase with her left hand. The younger Morland repeated the procedure with Bob The Cat. As we approached the door the man said, "Bringing some companions along today, I see."

"Yes we are. Aren't they adorable?" I couldn't have agreed more. We proceeded a short distance to one of the little airplanes. The Morlands carried us up a little stairway and through the open door of the plane. It was designed to seat six humans, two of them being the pilot and the copilot, in three rows of two seats each. We were soon settled in on two laps in the middle row. The pilot marched up the stairs and sat down in the seat on the left in the front row. He pushed a button and the stairway tilted up and sealed the opening through which we had entered. A door that doubles as a stairway, I thought, how clever. Humans have their moments.

The pilot fiddled with some more controls and the two propellers began to spin to the whine of the engines. The plane rolled down the runway, the ride getting bumpier and bumpier as we picked up speed. Just as I was thinking this was going to be worse than riding the city bus, the ride became smooth as silk as we lifted up into the air. It was quite pleasant, this sailing through the air among the clouds. Of course, that was too good to last.

"Looks like we're in for a little turbulence," said the pilot. "Make sure your seat belts are fastened." Well I had no idea what a turbulence was, but I didn't much like the sound of it. Then all of a sudden everything started shaking and bouncing around. Mrs. Morland did her best to hold onto me but I went flying out of her lap and bounced off the ceiling. When I came back down I missed her lap and landed on the floor, on my feet of course. I decided this was definitely worse than riding the city bus. I looked over to find that Bob The Cat was also on the floor. He was attempting to grasp the thin carpeting with his paws, an exercise in futility considering that, like the rest of us, he'd been declawed as a youngster. After the plane had bumped and bounced and swayed and rattled for what was probably only a few minutes, though it seemed longer, we were back to smooth sailing.

"Are you okay, kitty cat?" Mrs. Morland gently picked me up and placed me back in her lap. Bob The Cat, looking somewhat rattled by the experience, was back in Emma's lap. Out the little windows on the side of the plane I could see the clouds that we had just flown through. Apparently clouds and airplanes don't mix. The rest of the flight was uneventful, that is, until we reached our destination and it was time for the landing. The landing was enough to make me reconsider taking the bus with the dog on the side. At first it wasn't so bad. I could feel myself nudge forward a little as the plane began to slow down. Then it felt like we were falling, and the human passengers started fiddling with their seat belts to make sure they were snug enough. Mrs. Morland wrapped both of her arms around me, which I didn't mind at all considering that the alternative would likely be hitting the ceiling again. Then the little airplane started to shake and wiggle and lean back and forth. Just when I was getting used to all the motion we touched down, although *slammed* down would be more accurate. The tires let out a squeal and the plane bounced back up, then hit the pavement again. The process repeated itself a few of more times before the plane settled down on the runway. Just when I was ready to exhale, the pilot must have slammed on the brakes because the lady had to hold on even tighter to keep me from crashing into the back of the unoccupied copilot's seat. I looked over at Bob The Cat. He looked absolutely terrified. So much for flying.

The two Morland women remained perfectly calm through the whole ordeal, as if being tossed around like a rag doll was an everyday occurrence in their lives. The pilot, also looking not the least bit affected, got up and opened up the door that doubled as a stairway. Bob The Cat and I were carried down to the runway, and then something thoroughly unexpected happened. The humans put us down on the tarmac, took up their luggage, and proceeded on their way. By all appearances they were to be abandoned right then and there.

"That's odd," said Bob The Cat. And odd it was, because during our time on their laps practicing focused purring we had also suggested they drive us around town and help us find the cats.

"Very odd indeed," I replied. "They seem to have forgotten all about us. Come on, let's follow them. Maybe it's just a temporary distraction." We followed the humans into a little terminal building that looked pretty much like the one we had left behind in our town. Emma

Morland whipped an electronic device out of her purse and began talking into it, advising someone somewhere of their arrival.

"The car will be here in about twenty minutes," said Emma to her mother. Then she walked over to a snack bar, but instead of milk she purchased two cups of coffee. As Emma set down the coffees on a round table surrounded by cheap plastic chairs, Mrs. Morland was busy snatching various brochures, pamphlets, fliers, and catalogs from a display rack that stood against the wall near the main entrance. She spread the paperwork on the table, sat down, and began to stir cream and sugar into one of the cups of coffee.

"Let's see," said Emma, rearranging some of the pamphlets and brochures, "we can have James drop us off at the art gallery downtown. The other shops are close by." In minutes they had devised a strategy for attacking three jewelry stores, five shoe stores and four clothing boutiques. There was no mention of cats. It seemed that thoughts of shopping sprees had rendered our focused purring ineffective.

"So what do we do?" asked Bob The Cat, "start walking?"

"It might come to that, but let's hang around here for a while. We still might be able to catch a ride with them." We huddled under the table waiting for the humans to make a move. Once or twice I tried rubbing up against a leg in hope of at least getting a dish of milk. My efforts of course were in vain, the owner of the leg still preoccupied with the items of retail propaganda. Eventually the humans gathered their things and strolled across the terminal, which was a somewhat busier place than the baby airport terminal back home. Bob The Cat and I followed as they headed for the glass doors that I took to be the main entrance. These doors opened when one or more humans approached and stepped on one of the rubber mats placed directly in front of the doors. We followed them outside and when the two ladies stopped at the curb and set down their suitcases, Bob The Cat and I sat down right next to them. They still didn't seem to notice us.

Instead of a taxicab the car that showed up was a long black limousine. The driver, presumably James, was attired in a black uniform and cap just like the chauffeurs that drive the rich folks around in the movies. He quickly walked around and opened a door on the passenger side, the one toward the rear of the car that is, there being several doors on each side. Then James proceeded to relieve the ladies of their suitcases, giving us an opportunity to hop through the door and into the interior of the limousine. Compared to any car I had ever been in the interior of this one was rather spacious. There was not one but two rear seats, arranged so as to face each other. Between the seats was a coffee table which provided us with a convenient hiding place. Not that we needed to hide, the ladies being oblivious to our existence, but we crawled under there anyway because we're cats and that's just the sort of thing we like to do. Emma and Mrs. Morland soon got in and sat side by side in the back seat, spreading the catalogs and other material out on the coffee table. The car began to move and Bob The Cat and I settled in for a little nap.

The opening of the car door woke us. James was busy holding the door open and smiling and nodding, allowing us to slip out. The street was not unlike a downtown street in our town. Shops, restaurants, and offices lined both sides of the street. The only difference was that none of them seemed to be vacant. The women, followed by the chauffeur, entered one of the stores by way of one of those silly revolving doors. Bob The Cat wasn't the least bit tempted to mess with that door. Eventually the three humans reappeared one by one. James, bringing up the rear as usual, was carrying a couple of hat boxes and a large shopping bag. After depositing these items into the trunk of the limousine he hurried to catch up with the two shoppers, who were about to enter a department store just down the street. We waited around until they emerged from that store, James loaded down with even more merchandise. The Morlands continued on to another store.

Reasoning that this could go on for some time, I suggested we grab some lunch. Need I tell you that my brother thought it a capital idea? Circling around to the alleyway that ran behind the buildings, we managed to find the rear door of a restaurant that was left wide open. The only thing preventing our entry was a weathered screen door. The frame was warped and the hinges worn, causing the door to not quite close all the way. It was easily opened by the paw of a cat. Sneaking around inside, we could see that this was no fast food joint but rather a full service restaurant and an upscale one at that. It seems the humans don't keep their expensive restaurant kitchens any cleaner than the cheap ones. We feasted on scraps of scallops, rainbow trout, and crab meat. I even nibbled on a bit of salad. I'll try anything once.

"So what now?"

"I suppose we go look for the two women," I replied. I was watching the tuxedoed waiters coming and going through a pair of swinging doors that they deftly opened with a tap of a toe. "But what do you say we check out the dining room first? Maybe we can snatch some dessert."

"You don't have to ask me twice," he replied as he scampered off toward the door. He timed his run perfectly and disappeared into the dining room on the heels of a waiter who was carrying a large tray. I followed the next waiter through and found myself in a room full of tables covered in white tablecloths. Nearly all of the tables were occupied but the room wasn't noisy, the sound of numerous conversations dampened by the low ceiling and thick carpeting. The room was softly lit with little lamps on the tables supplementing the mood lighting subtly placed in recesses in the walls.

16) The Mansion

At a table for two across the room Emma and her mother sat perusing their menus, which were undoubtedly the dessert menus based on the fact that the waiter was busy removing their lunch plates. Bob The Cat and I ran across the room toward their table, carefully avoiding the uniformed personnel who were walking briskly around in all directions. We sat down underneath the table, fairly well hidden by the tablecloth.

"Let's see if I can get their attention," I whispered, and began to rub up against a leg and purr heartily. To my relief the shopping spree trance had been broken and Emma lifted up the tablecloth to peek under the table.

"Look, mother, it's our friends the cats."

"Nice kitties." Mrs. Morland lifted up the tablecloth and started petting Bob The Cat. Then she and her daughter simultaneously reached under the table, each grabbing a cat. We sat there on their laps and when dessert arrived they graciously shared with us.

"Madam, cats are not allowed in the dining room!" said a man in a tuxedo who had sidled up to our table. He purported to be the *maître d'*, whatever that is. "It's not only an annoyance to our other guests but a health code violation as well. Kindly remove them at once."

"Cats? What cats? I don't see any cats," said Emma with exaggerated innocence. She deftly slipped a wad of paper money into his hand as she spoke. She had obviously chosen the correct denominations because the man nodded and backed away from the table with a smile on his face.

"Home, James," said Mrs. Morland. The women had carried us back to the limousine. Bob the cat was seated on Emma's lap, I on her mother's. The chauffeur turned at the next corner and guided the car up a tree-lined boulevard and then made another right turn. As if by magic a wrought iron gate split down the middle and the two halves swung backwards to make way for the limousine. I noticed a sign on the side of the entryway that simply said *private*. We proceeded up a long gravel driveway through a manicured lawn dotted with neatly trimmed shrubbery and trees. The house we pulled up to was by far the biggest and certainly the oldest one I had ever seen. It was all red brick with columns and gables and ivy clinging to the walls. There was a three-story section in the middle with a large entryway and massive double doors for the main entrance. Protruding from the main structure were two-story wings on either side, the ends of which seemed to extend into the surrounding woods. Somehow I got the impression there was a lot more to be seen behind the facade. Obviously these Morland folks were loaded.

As Bob The Cat and I were being carried into the house, James opened the trunk in order to unload the suitcases and various boxes and bags containing the purchases from the shopping spree. The big doors opened and a man dressed in a black suit stood at attention as we entered.

"It will just be Emma and I for dinner at seven, Jeeves." Have James pick up some cat food, the good stuff in the little cans. And some kitty litter, too."

"Very well, ma'am," said the man in the black suit, nodding slightly.

The front doors opened into a large foyer with a high ceiling and what was surely a marble floor. Two stairways on either side curved upward to a landing that stretched across the room. The hand railings on the stairs and the upstairs balustrade were thick and solid looking. We were taken down a carpeted hallway and into a room that was reminiscent of the library in Gramps' house. This one was larger of course, and there were a couple of desks on which sat computers. Our hosts were engaged in a discussion about their investment portfolio. It seems that due to the simultaneous maturing of several bonds they found themselves in possession of a larger than ordinary amount of cold hard cash. A nice problem to have if you ask me.

"Now you two stay put," said Mrs. Morland as she and Emma gently dropped us onto the carpet. "We'll be back in no time with something for you to eat." To insure that we stayed put, they closed the door behind them.

"I've got an idea," I said as soon as they were gone. I explained to Bob The Cat how Ben Bennett's car dealership was tanking and how it looked like they wouldn't be able to afford to send Mary Ann to rocket science school.

"And you figure the Morlands will take it off his hands."

"Exactly," I replied.

"Won't you feel bad when these nice ladies are stuck with such a crummy investment?" Try as he might, my brother could not keep a straight face for long. We both had a good laugh.

A few minutes later Emma entered the room followed by a middle-aged woman wearing what I took to be some kind of a domestic servant's uniform, which looked like a cross between a waitress uniform and a square dancer's dress. The servant was carrying a tray which she carefully placed on the floor in the middle of the room, revealing its contents to be two dishes of the most scrumptious canned cat food, two dishes of milk, and two dishes of water. We thanked our hostess with a couple of meows and dug right in. After we had stuffed ourselves, Bob The Cat and I curled up on the sofa. While we were eating someone had placed a litter box on the floor and shut the door behind them. It seems we were not to have the run of the house. No matter, we slept until about midnight.

"You awake?"

"I am now," I replied with a yawn.

"What do you say we go look for the cats from our litter?"

"Sure, why not?"

"Shall we do the purring thing and get the ladies to drive us around town?"

I thought about it for a moment and then replied, "I think we might have a better look on foot. Besides, I could use some exercise, couldn't you?"

We weren't about to get that door open, so I climbed up on a credenza that was conveniently situated beneath a window. "Looks like they left this one cracked open for ventilation. Come on, if we both push I think we can open it enough to get out."

And out the window we went and across the lawn. Of course we had no clue as to where to begin to look, but we weren't about to let that stop us. After passing through the gate we went from house to house and neighborhood to neighborhood letting out frequent inquisitive meows. We managed to make friends with a few of the cats in town, who promised to get the word out that the two cats from down south were searching for their siblings. It was dawn by the time we slipped back in through the window and sacked out on the sofa again.

"Wake up, kitties," said Mrs. Morland, "it's time for your breakfast!" At that she entered the room, followed by Emma and then the servant who was once again carrying a tray full of treats for us. This time instead of leaving us in peace to dine, the humans sat on the sofa and watched us eat, which seemed to fascinate them to no end. Of course when we were through we curled up in their laps for some more focused purring. Soon they were not only convinced that the day's business would be to purchase an automobile dealership in a certain town to the south, but this time they would have James drive them and take the cats along for the ride.

The agreed-upon time of departure was two hours away, so Bob The Cat and I slipped out the window again and visited a couple of the friends we had made the night before. So far there weren't any leads, which was not too surprising considering the fact that we weren't even a hundred percent sure that we had the right town in the first place. We left word that they should expect a visit from two cats named Princess and Soldier in the days to come.

Climbing back into the mansion through the window, we had time for a quick nap before it was time to board the limousine. We made a stop in what was certainly the downtown area, in front of a large two-story red brick house. It reminded me of the house where Gramps lives. From the sign in front I could see that it now housed law offices.

"I won't be long, dear," said Mrs. Morland, stepping out of the car as James held the door open. She followed the short walkway to the three steps that led to a generous wrap-around porch complete with a porch swing. I wondered if the lawyers ever found time to sit on it. She was true to her word, emerging only a few minutes later accompanied by a woman attired in a beige knee-length skirt and a matching jacket over a pastel blouse. The woman, her attorney I assumed, handed her a legal-size manila folder.

"Everything should be in order. Mr. Bennett is expecting you."

"Thank you for getting this ready on such short notice. I really appreciate it."

"Don't mention it. I was glad to do it for my old... er, most valued client." Good save. "Let me know if you have any questions."

I was a bit nervous when we passed a retail mall on the way out of town, but the Morlands were too focused on the purchase of the dealership to be tempted to do any more shopping. The drive, of course, was substantially more time consuming than flying. Bob The Cat curled up on the floor beneath the little coffee table for a nap. I was curious to see the scenery go by so I stood up on one of the seats, my front paws on the window sill. Emma and her mother seemed to think this was the most adorable thing they had ever seen. After a while I got bored with watching the trees and cows go by so I too had a little nap.

It was late afternoon when the limousine pulled into the parking lot of Ben Bennett's car dealership. I figured as soon as the door opened we would walk over to the next bus stop and catch a ride home. Before James could open the door, Emma had a firm grip on me and Bob The Cat was in Mrs. Morland's arms. We were carried past the rows of shiny new cars, the signs in the windshields touting automatic transmissions, air conditioning, leather seats, state of the art sound systems and low, *low, LOW!!!* prices. The facade of the building was all floor-to-ceiling glass with signs informing anyone who cared to look that here were the absolute best bargains to be had in the automotive world.

We were taken straight into the office. The windowless room contained some filing cabinets, a few chairs, and a coffee table, but these were dwarfed by the massive oak desk behind which sat Mr. Bennett. The walls were covered in wood paneling with a few pieces of generic artwork hanging here and there. You got the feeling that he had meant to finish decorating but just never got around to it.

"Hello, I've been expecting you," he said, rising quickly from his executive leather swivel chair, "did you have a pleasant flight?"

"We usually fly, but drove down this time. Don't ask me why, it just seemed like the thing to do. I'm Emma and this is my mother, Anne."

"A pleasure to make your acquaintance." Ben shook hands with Emma and then Mrs. Morland. I suppose I could call her Anne now that I know her first name. "Please, have a seat. Would you like some coffee? Or a soft drink?"

"Coffee would be nice."

"Yes, the same for me."

The visitors sat down on two chairs that were conveniently placed directly in front of the big desk. Bob The Cat and I took our places, one of us on each lap.

"Brought the pets, I see," said Ben, smiling. "Funny, they look just like two of our cats. I'll be right back." He hurried out of the room and returned shortly carrying a small tray on which rested two polystyrene foam cups along with some packets of sugar, sugar substitute, and powdered cream. Seems to me a big shot car dealer and former mayoral candidate ought to have someone to fetch coffee for him, but what do I know?

"You are aware," said Ben, looking serious, "of the possibility of an IRS audit."

"Oh that?" Anne made a careless waving motion with her hand, as if to dismiss the subject as entirely unimportant. "Don't worry about that. We've got friends in high places." Must be nice. I don't know how these things usually go, but it seemed to me that the business was done very quickly. When Anne disclosed the purchase price they were offering for the dealership, Ben's face lit up like a kid's on Christmas morning. I was willing to bet that it would be more than enough to send Mary Ann to rocket science school. Just as I was thinking it was time Bob The Cat and I made a break for it, Anne spoke.

"James, take us to the Pinewood Mall." Turning to her daughter, she said, "Emma, there's some pretty good retail space there that's renting dirt cheap. I was thinking we could open a shop or two there." Might as well ride over to the mall with them, I thought, since it's easier to catch the bus home from there.

The limousine pulled up to the shopping mall entrance and James opened the door. Bob The Cat and I hopped out and hid under the car. Neither Mrs. Morland nor Emma made any effort to stop us, their attention having been drawn to several signs in a store window advertising a big sale in bold red letters. We followed the humans through the entrance. They turned left and we turned right, intending to see what was up at the disco food court. There we found more of the usual activity, teenagers dancing to the disco beat. Their moves seemed to be improving, practice making perfect. After a while we tired of the scene and decided to head for home, but not before snacking on some scraps at the fish and chips shop.

We crept along the mall past the store fronts, every other one of which was vacant. It was devoid of any life until we reached the far end, where there were a number of rather nicely dressed humans milling around.

"Looks like something going on down there," I said. "What do you say we investigate?"

"Yeah, why not?"

We approached the little crowd of humans and found a hiding place behind a trash can. I peeked out long enough to read the sign above the entrance to the store front where the humans were gathered. It read:

Grand Opening – Pinewood Art Gallery

Before long the doors were opened and the humans drifted in, doing their best to look as aloof and disinterested as possible. We followed them in and found a dimly lit corner from which we could witness the proceedings.

"That's considered his best work, although I'm partial to *Fountain in Marseilles* myself." I recognized the voice as that of Emma Morland. She stood next to none other than Pete, Mary Ann's ex-boyfriend. He was admiring a painting that hung on the wall adjacent to our corner. Emma was admiring him. Go figure.

"Abstractions do nothing for me. Nothing at all." The voice belonged to a woman in an expensive-looking dress accompanied by a man in a tuxedo. "This I can at least relate to."

The man was wearing a name tag that identified him as the proprietor of the establishment. They were admiring the same painting Pete had been looking at, he and Emma having moved on to a sculpture in the center of the room that appeared human-like, except for its lack of limbs of any kind.

"Couldn't agree with you more. Surrealism, however, I can live with. A melted watch, yes. A melted nothing, no." Suddenly the woman turned and took a step toward us. Bob The Cat and I instinctively froze.

"What lovely sculptures," she said, bending down to observe us closely. "So lifelike."

"Yes, very rare pieces, these. We were lucky to find them. Very rare." Liar.

"Why don't you display them somewhere more prominent, with better lighting?"

"No, we couldn't do that. The artist insisted they be displayed this way, in a dark corner. Like they're watching us, and don't want to be seen." Yeah, right.

17) The Mutt

Once we had had enough of the art scene, the two of us had an uneventful bus ride back to the neighborhood.

"Clarence! Whiskers! Where have you two been?" said Mary Ann as she saw us emerge through the pet door. I could have answered, but chose not to. I made a mental note to take the first opportunity to use some focused purring in order to inform her of Bob The Cat's proper name. *Whiskers* my foot!

All of a sudden a cacophony of ear-piercing banging, clanging, crashing, rapping, tapping, thumping and whomping filled the air. I could feel the hair on my back stick straight up and observe the same happening to my brother. After the initial shock, our cat curiosity won out over the instinct to flee. We crept toward the racket, which seemed to be emanating from the back bedroom.

"Who gives a five-year-old a drum set?" I said out loud, although no one including myself could hear the words. Back out the pet door we ran and hopped onto the cinder block wall. I scurried toward Soldier's house with Bob The Cat right on my tail. Soldier was home and Princess was there too.

"Hey, look who's back," she said. "How did it go?"

"I'm afraid there's no sign of our siblings," I replied, "but we did manage to sell Ben's car dealership at a tidy profit. As soon as the check clears, the Bennett's will have more than enough dough to send Mary Ann to rocket science school. Which is a good thing, what with the ruby necklace surely destroyed in the fire."

"That's terrific. I just hope she can take me with her when she leaves for school. By the way, have you been home yet?"

"Oh yeah. Who gives a five year old a drum set anyway?"

"Soldier has already done a little focused purring on his owner so you guys can stay here as long as necessary. The human has already been to the store to buy extra cat food."

"That's a relief. It shouldn't last too long, though. Humans get bored with their new toys pretty quickly, especially at that age."

"Hey, I've got an idea," said Princess with mischief in her eyes. "Now that Ben's got some extra cash, we do some focused purring and get him to use some of it to start a gourmet cat food business. And we'll be the taste testers!" This proposition, I hardly need to tell you, met with unanimous approval.

Our joy, however, was to be short lived. A few days later Princess, Bob The Cat and I were back home, the drumming having ceased at least temporarily. Ben came home with some bad news.

"The deal fell through."

"What do you mean, *fell through*?" Betty turned from the German chocolate cake she was busy frosting. It looked good.

"It fell through," replied Ben, opening the refrigerator door. He stood there a moment and then shut it. "As in canceled. Not happening. Over and done with."

"But how? They were paying cash weren't they? How could it fall through?"

"There's an appraisal clause in the contract. Says the buyer can void the deal if an independent appraisal places the value of the business at less than a certain percentage of the purchase price. And trust me, it came in *way* under. I guess I should have known it was too good to be true."

Once again it looked like it was going to be junior college for Mary Ann. Princess, Bob The Cat, and I sat on the front porch, our little cat brains devoid of any idea as to what to try next. Suddenly Bob The Cat stood up, squinting to have a look at a critter coming up the street.

"What's that?" I said, "A dog?"

"Yeah, but just a little one. Nothing to worry about."

"Doesn't it look familiar to you?" asked Princess.

"Hey, the little mutt managed to escape from the fire." The dog galloped towards us across the front lawn and made a sudden turn just before he reached the porch, making for the back yard.

"Look!" said Princess, "He's got the ruby necklace!"

"Let's get him!" I said, and the three of us gave chase. Roscoe and Muffin happened to be playing in the back yard. The dog began to run around in circles on the back lawn with the kittens following close behind. When it slowed down for a moment to have a look at the kittens, Muffin pounced on its back. She proceeded to ride the little dog like a cowboy on a bucking bronco with Roscoe running along right on its heels. Eventually the little dog got tired and we had it surrounded, managing to relieve him of the jewelry without a fight. Apparently he was tired of carrying the thing around.

"Let's keep him," said Princess, "I've always wanted a pet."

"Yeah," said Bob The Cat, "maybe we can teach it to talk." We had a good laugh over that comment. While Bob The Cat fed the little mutt some of the expensive cat food and Princess deposited the ruby necklace onto Mary Ann's night stand, I ran over to Gramps' house to grab the magazine with the photograph of the DuRaques and the necklace. When the Bennetts read the article and realized the necklace was in their possession, they were so excited that it never dawned on them to wonder how the old magazine landed on the coffee table in their living room.

The next morning a big black limousine pulled up in front of the Bennett house. This one was longer than the Morlands' car, and looked newer and shinier. It not only had a chauffeur, but a second uniformed human who opened the door for the single passenger. The passenger was male, tall, and sun tanned, his blonde hair suggestive of California surfer dudes. The human was attired casually but expensively, as if his next stop was the country club for a round of golf. Walking briskly up the drive and over to the front porch, he paused just long enough to pat Bob The Cat on the head before ringing the doorbell.

"Mister DuRaque?" said Mary Ann with a smile as she opened the front door. "It's a pleasure to meet you. Won't you come in?"

"Thank you. And call me Fitz."

"Fritz? Like Fritz The Cat?"

"Without the 'R'. Fitz, short for Fitzwilliam."

Princess managed to slip inside before the door shut. Bob The Cat and I had to scamper around to the back yard and enter through the pet door. Introductions were still being made when we arrived in the living room, the entire family making it a point to be home for the occasion. The visitor was escorted into the den and refreshments were served. My feline friends and I patiently waited for a chance to grab some for ourselves.

"This is it," said the visitor, "my grandmother's ruby necklace. There's no other like it." Mary Ann handed him the necklace which he held gently, almost reverently.

"Once we found out what it was, we wanted to make sure it was returned to its rightful owner," said Betty. "How it came into our possession is a mystery."

"My son Joey here found it in a box of family photos and keepsakes," added Ben. "And then what did you do with it, Joey?"

"Gave it to Mary Ann," said the boy, "For her birthday."

"Well, I want to thank you all for your honesty. You could have gotten a fair chunk of change at any pawn shop for this. The sentimental value to my family, though, is impossible to put a price on. If there's anything I can do for you..."

"Mary Ann wants to go to school but can't afford it." The words were out of Joey's mouth before anyone could stop him.

"Joey," said Betty, "we can't ask Mr. DuRaque to pay for Mary Ann's college. That's a lot of money."

"Which college are you interested in, Mary Ann? Seriously, I want to reward you. Don't worry about the cost, I can afford it. Did you see that car parked outside? A driver *and* a door man. I don't mean to brag, I'm just sayin'."

"Well," said Mary Ann sheepishly, "if you really want to know."

"I really want to know."

"I want to study rocket science. At I.R.S., the Institute..."

"Of rocket science."

"You know the school?" asked Max.

"Know it? I'm on the board of directors. I love rockets! I fly down to the cape whenever I can to watch them launch a big one. So how are your grades?" he asked, turning to Mary Ann.

"Good enough to get in. Not good enough for a scholarship."

"They're good enough now. As of this moment you're awarded a full scholarship. Four years of tuition, room, and board."

Just then the doorbell rang. Mr. and Mrs. Bennett both got up at the same time, but Ben sat back down when his wife gestured for him to stay put. She went over to the front door, still smiling from the good news. After a moment she returned and whispered something to Mary Ann, who responded by shaking her head. Her mother gave her a look that seemed to say that Mary Ann would be expected to talk to the person at the door, whoever it was.

"Oh all right," she said aloud, walking reluctantly toward the door. I followed, of course. "What do you want?" The person at the door was Pete, wearing his ice cream shop uniform. The lack of stains on his apron told me that he was on his way to work.

"I came to apologize for missing the Fowl Ball. I'm sorry, really I am. But I did have to work that night." Pete was either genuinely sorry or a pretty good actor.

"Well, okay. I forgive you. But we're not getting back together. I'm going away to school, and even if I was staying in town I wouldn't have time for you anyway." She saw the pained expression on Pete's face and quickly added, "Or any other guy for that matter."

18) The School

The time came for Mary Ann to leave for school. Princess and I sat on the floor in her room, watching her select items of clothing from her closet and dresser. She neatly folded each item and arranged them in the large suitcase that lay open on her bed.

"Be right there," she shouted in response to a request by her mother to help in the kitchen. As soon as Mary Ann had left the room, Princess hopped onto the bed, padded across the bedspread, and crawled into the suitcase. She looked so cozy and contented on her bed of apparel that I decided to join her.

"Princess! Clarence!" We must have dozed off because we didn't hear Mary Ann return to the bedroom. "All right, out you go," she said as she picked Princess up and deposited her on the floor. I tried crawling under a pair of slacks, but she captured me as well. Not much room to hide in a suitcase. Well, as soon as she put me down Princess crawled right back in, and then as soon she removed Princess I crawled right back in. And so it went for a while, but eventually Mary Ann tired of our little game. She picked Princess and I up, one in each arm, and unceremoniously dumped us into the hallway, finishing up her packing behind closed doors. Well, behind one closed door anyway.

The next morning the future rocket scientist said her goodbyes to her father and brothers. Mrs. Bennett opened the trunk of her car and placed a suitcase inside. Princess had run off with Soldier to look for mice, and Roscoe and

Muffin were nowhere to be seen, leaving Bob The Cat and I to sit on the porch wondering what kind of trouble we could get ourselves into.

"What do you say we tag along with Mary Ann?" said Bob The Cat. "I've never been to a school before." It sounded like a good idea to me, so we crept under the car and waited for the doors to open. Soon we were riding down the highway, making ourselves comfortable on the floor behind the front seats. I took the opportunity to take a nap. When the car came to a stop and Mary Ann and Mrs. Bennett got out, Bob The Cat and I hopped out and hid under the car while Mary Ann retrieved her suitcase from the trunk. I could see the entrance to an impressive-looking building over which was inscribed:

As a matter of fact, it IS rocket science!

We waited until the humans had traversed the asphalt of the parking lot to enter the building, then turned our attention to the first order of business: food.

"Let's try that building over there," I said. "It looks like a cafeteria." Circling around to the rear, we spotted a door propped open. Nearby a couple of men dressed in white from head to toe were having a cigarette break. What is it about food service occupations that make humans want to smoke so much? I slipped through the opening with Bob The Cat right on my tail. Inside there were several others also dressed in white. Chefs, cooks, and their assistants, no doubt!

"There's our test subjects." The voice belonged to a woman with neatly trimmed medium-length reddish-brown hair. She wore glasses and was holding a clipboard. "Come along now," she said as she picked Bob The Cat up with her free hand. "Frank, grab the other cat." One of the smokers hurried into the room and grabbed me. I could have easily eluded him, but why would I want to miss out on a taste test? Obviously they were expecting a couple of cats on whom to try out some recipes, weren't they? If the other two couldn't show up on time it's their loss.

We were taken right back out the door and into a large white van. The human called Frank handed me off to another white-clad individual, the sous chef I supposed, and sat down in the driver's seat. The further we drove the more convinced I was that we were in for a real treat. I figured it must be a very special recipe if they had gone to this much trouble to ensure secrecy. When we arrived at our destination Bob The Cat and I were whisked into an elevator which must have taken us up to at least the twelfth floor. The elevator door opened to reveal a smallish room occupied by more white-clad humans. By then my mouth was watering in anticipation of the meal of a lifetime!

Hindsight is twenty-twenty, but I really should have known something wasn't quite right when Bob The Cat and I were taken into a tiny room and strapped snugly into a couple of contraptions that looked like those car seats that humans haul their babies around in. I mean, really, why the need to make us prisoners if they were about to serve us a delicious meal? At the time though, my thinking was clouded by all the salivating over the imaginary feast.

The little door to the tiny room was closed on us and there we were, all tied up and no food.

"Let's get out of here," I said.

Bob The Cat didn't reply, his teeth already busy chewing on the straps. I started chewing too, and we kept at it for what seemed like a very long time but was actually probably only five minutes. At that point we heard what sounded like a clap of thunder. Then the little room began to shake and a couple of seconds later I felt myself pressed against the seat. I noticed there was a small window over on Bob The Cat's side of the room. I could see a tower next to us, no doubt containing the elevator that brought us there, sinking into the ground. Then it dawned on me that the tower was standing still and we were being lifted up into the air.

"This is no dining room!" I exclaimed over the roar of the rocket engines. "We're in a space capsule!"

"On top of a rocket!" added my companion unnecessarily.

I felt myself being pushed back against the car seat, gaining weight without having had a bite to eat. Eventually the noise of the rocket ceased and out the window I could see the spent rocket falling back to Earth. By now Bob The Cat had freed himself from the car seat and was floating around in the cabin. I felt rather light and after a little more gnawing at the straps I was floating free as well. It was a bit unnerving at first. I mean, how are we supposed to land on our feet if we don't land? I was just getting used to it and beginning to enjoy the experience when a green light on what looked like a control panel began to flash on and off. I did my best to ignore it, but it just kept on flashing, faster and faster, brighter and brighter. I noticed there was a button of sorts next to the light so I punched it with my paw, figuring what did I have to lose? Well lo and behold, a tiny door opened and out floated a food pellet. It didn't look particularly appetizing, but the proof of the pudding being in the eating, I snatched it out of the air and scarfed it down.

"How did you do that?" My companion of course had smelled it. By the way, it had a seafood smell to it (scallops perhaps) and taste-wise wasn't bad at all for a food pellet. Not that I possessed any frame of reference for judging the quality or lack thereof of space-capsule food pellets.

"I pushed that button." Bob The Cat, of course, immediately punched the button. Nothing happened. "I think you have to wait for the light to flash," I said. After a few seconds the light resumed its flashing and he punched the button and got fed.

So there we were, two cats in space, floating around and happily munching on food pellets.

19) The Ship

Just as Bob The Cat and I were getting used to space travel, floating around munching on food pellets being not such a bad way to spend an afternoon, we were suddenly slammed against our little car seats. It seems the retro rockets had fired and we were about to begin the fiery descent back to Earth. I knew this from having seen a documentary on Animal Planet about a monkey who had been subjected to the same traumatic experience some years ago.

"Better hang onto what's left of your seat belt," I said, "it could be bumpy." By the time the words had left my mouth Bob The Cat was already holding on for dear life. The descent wasn't half as bad as our flight on the Morlands' baby airplane, but the sight of flames streaming by the little window was a bit unnerving. I was sure glad to see the candy-cane striped parachutes open up to gently lower us to the ground. Except there wasn't any ground. We were unceremoniously dumped into a body of water, our little capsule bobbing up and down with the waves.

"This thing sure makes a lousy boat," said my companion, who was beginning to look as if he'd swallowed some rancid fish. It might have been my imagination, but I'm telling you he turned just a bit greenish.

"Yeah," I replied, "I hope they don't plan on leaving us out here for very long." We bobbed around for a while in what I by then had concluded must be the ocean. There just aren't waves that big in lakes. Soon I was feeling a bit green myself.

"Sea monster! Sea monster!" shrieked Bob The Cat. He was referring to the masked human in a rubber diving suit who was peering into our little window.

"Relax," I said. He's here to take us to the recovery ship. And then, hopefully, feed us." At this my brother settled down a bit. Momentarily the hatch popped open and we were lifted into a basket of sorts that was hanging by a rope that extended up to the sky. The other end was attached to a helicopter noisily hovering overhead. I closed my eyes as we were being hoisted upward toward the helicopter, finding the sight of all that water below us rather unnerving. When we got there we had to be pried out of the basket, so tightly were we holding on. Eventually I opened my eyes to find I was sitting on the lap of a human who was sitting next to the pilot. Bob The Cat was stretched out on the pilot's lap, looking curiously at the various knobs and buttons within reach. I shot him a look that said *don't you dare touch anything*. There were ample windows to provide a view of the ocean in several directions. Not that anything in any direction looked any different from anything in any other direction. It was just water, water everywhere. Except for the big gray ship on the horizon straight ahead, that is.

We made a surprisingly smooth touchdown on the deck of the ship, which turned out to be roughly the size of a small country. There were numerous uniformed humans lined up to greet us with a generous round of applause. We were taken directly to a room with lots of stainless steel cabinets and surfaces. On many of the surfaces stood various scientific-looking instruments and contraptions. The uniformed humans who had carried us from the helicopter unceremoniously plopped us down on one of the stainless steel surfaces. There were several more humans awaiting us, these attired in white lab coats.

"Where are the collars?" demanded one of the lab coats, his gaze directed at the uniformed one who had been holding Bob The Cat.

"What collars?"

"The data collars! The ones they were wearing! We can't retrieve the data without the collars!" Speaking of collars, he was getting a bit hot under his.

"They weren't wearing them when we picked them up." Turning to the other uniformed one, he barked, "Go check the capsule for the collars. They've got to be in there somewhere."

The chief lab coat began to pace back and forth across the room, looking more agitated by the minute. He kept muttering mostly unintelligible syllables to himself, but I could make out "collars", "expensive", and "big trouble" among other niceties.

"Sorry," said the uniform when he returned after a while. "There are no collars. We checked everywhere. Unless they ate them." At this he gently scratched me between the ears and said, "You wouldn't eat the nasty collars, now would you, nice kitty."

The chief lab coat then picked up a telephone that was attached to a nearby wall and screamed "Get me headquarters. NOW!" He was turning red and looking about as tense as a human can get. I was beginning to wonder if we might be witnesses to the explosion of an actual human head. After a minute he once again screamed into the phone, "What do you mean they're the wrong cats?"

After this episode we were fed our fill of the expensive canned cat food washed down with fresh bowls of milk. Then we were taken to a little room and put inside a cat carrier where we were left alone. The latch was easily opened and no one had bothered to shut the door to the room, so Bob The Cat and I decided we might as well wander around and enjoy ourselves. I had always wanted to take a cruise. We circled around the entirety of the ship's deck only to find that the view was pretty much the same in every direction. I never knew so much water existed. Eventually we made our way back to the cat carrier and got some sleep.

The next morning right after breakfast we were taken to a deck where our space capsule was on display. Next to it was a long table with several chairs which were occupied by humans in very fancy uniforms. Facing the table were humans with TV cameras and microphones. Bob The Cat and I were placed at the center of the table. One of the humans in the fancy uniforms began to speak.

"Thank you all for being here today. It's a pleasure to address the media after such a successful mission. Our specially trained cats here, Astro and Cosmo, performed as expected and brought back valuable data for our researchers at the Institute of Rocket Science." Liar. "Yes, ma'am," he added, pointing toward one of the humans with a microphone.

"Captain Elroy, the photo in the press kit clearly shows that Astro is a calico. This one is all white. What gives?"

"She's a bleach blond." Some of the media people began to jot down notes in their little notebooks. "Next question."

"Did the cats perform as well as you had hoped?"

"Absolutely, thanks to the excellent training they received at the Institute of Rocket Science."

"What have you learned from this flight?"

"It has confirmed our hypothesis that specially trained cats such as Astro and Cosmo can be valuable additions to the crew of a spacecraft on a long-term mission. Keeping the craft free of mice, providing companionship, and so on."

And so it went, the Captain lying through his teeth and the various members of the media lapping it up. Bob The Cat and I found it all very amusing.

Our sea cruise was short lived. The bogus press conference wrapped up and Bob The Cat and I were loaded back into the helicopter. We flew right back to where we had started, the Institute of Rocket Science. Mary Ann was waiting for the helicopter ready to claim us, having seen the press conference on TV.

"Clarence! Whiskers! What am I going to do with you two? Running off to outer space!" Our efforts to get Mary Ann to call Bob The Cat by his proper name had been ineffective. Sometimes humans just latch onto an idea and they just won't let go. She carried us, one in each arm, to her car and proceeded to drive us all the way home. It was nice to be back. Soldier, Gramps and Princess, along with Roscoe and Muffin, were in the back yard ready to welcome us home. They treated us as some sort of conquering heroes, quite unnecessarily, as we hadn't really done anything other than try to mooch a free meal. They obviously thought we had intentionally pulled off a space capsule hijacking. We didn't bother to disclose the truth right away, though, any excuse for a party being okay with us.

We were pleasantly surprised to see three cats approach and reveal themselves to be the others from our litter whom we had searched for in vain. They, too, had seen the press conference on TV. It turns out they had been living all this time on a farm just up the road from the now-burnt Route 58 Trading Post. Introductions were made and then Princess filled Bob The Cat and I in on what had been going on around town in our absence.

"You won't believe this," she said, clearly excited. "Emma and Pete, believe it or not, are getting married."

"Emma *Morland*? And Pete the ice cream guy?"

"It's true. Soldier and I overheard them making plans. With Emma's money and Pete's expertise they plan to purchase the ice cream parlor and then expand into a chain."

"You don't say."

"I *do* say," she replied, giving me a funny look. "And get this. The manager of the shopping mall was talking about removing the juke box from the food court. He was of the opinion that the teenagers, instead of attracting paying customers, tended to drive people away."

"Fortunately," interjected Soldier, "his wife is a cat person. We managed to find out where they live and showed up at the house looking hungry and pathetic. She took us in and fed us and, long story short, she talked him into changing his mind thanks to some expert focused purring on our part."

"Well done. I'm rather fond of the disco food court."

"Clarence," said Gramps rather seriously. It was late and the party had wound down. "Word of your triumphant flight has spread not only around the neighborhood but all over town and beyond. I believe this is the perfect opportunity to do something I've always dreamed of but never found the opportunity to pursue."

"Sounds big," I said. "What do you have in mind?"

"A gathering of the cats."

"Which cats? Isn't pretty much everyone here tonight?"

"Think big, Clarence. I mean a gathering of *all* the cats. Cats from near and far, from all over town and other towns, too!"

"Sounds… interesting."

"Why don't you come over tomorrow afternoon to discuss this? And bring Princess and Soldier." As an afterthought he added, "and what's his name, Bob, bring him too if you'd like."

"Bob The Cat."

"Right, Bob The Cat. Bring him too."

20) The Gathering

"This gathering, as I mentioned to Clarence last night, is something I've wanted to do for years." Gramps was addressing me, Princess, Soldier and Bob The Cat in the library. His human was out for the day, numerous errands suddenly needing his undivided attention due to some expert focused purring by Gramps. There were two other elderly cats present, one seated on either side of him. "The benefits of assembling all of us in one place are numerous. Training the younger ones in the art of focused purring is the most important, in my view. Also I believe we can form a network for the exchange of information regarding food supplies, potential human homes for strays and alley cats, and locations of vicious dogs. But where are my manners?" He proceeded to introduce us to the two elderly cats, Fluffy and Mister Meow. They were from the same litter as Gramps and had traveled some distance in order to meet with us.

Soldier raised his paw and waited for a nod from Gramps to begin speaking. "But how are we to get all of the cats together in one place? I don't have to tell you that we're not the most sociable of creatures."

"Easy," replied the old cat. "Word has already spread about the exploits of our very own space travelers, *cats*-tronauts Clarence and Bob The Cat. Plenty of cats will want to meet them, and the others will follow out of curiosity." I felt a bit uncomfortable with the idea of being the main attraction, having become a catstronaut quite by accident.

"It will easily be the largest gathering of cats in history," said Fluffy.

"But where will it be held?" asked Princess. "All those cats aren't going to fit in anyone's back yard."

"True, and with a yard full of cats the humans would panic anyway," said Mister Meow. "Gramps, fortunately, has found us the perfect venue, which is..." With that he deferred to our host.

"The golf course at the country club over on the edge of town. The club is closed on Mondays so there are no humans around except the grounds keeper and the lady who runs the office. I have it on good authority that they're both cat persons. In fact the maintenance man keeps his cat right there at the club. For reasons unknown to me he named her *Birdie*."

"I can see the advantages of gathering on a golf course," said Soldier, "plenty of room, all grassy and surrounded by shade trees. Not to mention plenty of water to drink at the water hazard. But where are we to get enough food for all these cats? There could be hundreds."

"It's already been arranged. A little focused purring by Birdie, the kitchen door is *accidentally* left open, we help ourselves!"

With all due respect to Gramps and the other elders, the gathering would turn out to be the worst idea since the Ford Edsel.

The whole gang, Roscoe and Muffin included, hopped aboard the bus early Monday morning. We reached downtown, transferred to Route Forty-Seven, and then walked the last quarter mile to the country club. There we found Gramps, Fluffy and Mister Meow on a terrace overlooking the golf course. Bob The Cat and I were directed to a nearby shady spot where we would await our introduction to the crowd. There was plenty of room so the others joined us. Cats were already arriving from all over town and beyond. There were old cats and young cats, thin cats and fat cats, black cats and white cats, calicos, Siamese and tabbies. There was even a small clowder of the very rare California Spangled accompanied by their bodyguards, a couple of big alley cats (the kind you don't mess with). By late morning the golf course was filled with felines. The first sign of the trouble to come was the way the cats were forming groups, everyone remaining with others of their own kind. Tabbies here, calicos there, and so on. Each breed was eying the others with suspicion, if not outright hostility. Various factions were jostling for position, the area closest to the kitchen door being the most sought after of course.

"That cat looks familiar," said Princess. "Where have I seen her before?" She was referring to a tabby who was fiddling with the club's public address system which had somehow been dragged out onto the terrace. I immediately recognized her as Tabitha of the French-fried time machine. At that moment the air was filled with a shriek the likes of which I had never heard. Cats everywhere jumped in the air, fur standing up and claws extended. This was accompanied by a cacophony of angry meows.

"Nothing to worry about folks, just a little feedback in the public address system." Mister Meow had stepped up to the microphone. He waited for the crowd to settle down and then continued, "thank you all for attending the inaugural Gathering Of The Cats. I know some of you have traveled from very far away to get here." This elicited some spirited meows from several groups. "Gramps will be here momentarily to deliver the opening address. After that we'll meet our brave space travelers, catstronauts Clarence and Bob The Cat. Meanwhile, the kitchen door is open so help yourselves to some grub."

The last comment, of course, resulted in swarms of cats converging on the kitchen. Just as the resulting cat fights were breaking out, a foursome of unauthorized golfers appeared at the first tee. The *thwack* of a nicely struck tee shot momentarily filled the air. Cats scrambled to get out of the way as the ball landed on the fairway and rolled toward the green. Authorized or not, one does not interfere with the game. The other three teed off, seemingly indifferent to all the cats running this way and that. As the golfers were traipsing down the fairway to search for their tiny spheres, a human was heard shouting.

"Hey you! Get off the golf course! We're CLOSED on Mondays!" It was the grounds keeper. He was barreling along on a riding lawn mower, chasing after the golfers and waving a large garden tool over his head. At this point complete chaos reigned. Cats were going berserk: rolling around in the sand traps, pouncing on the riding mower, and a couple of them climbing up the pants legs of the unauthorized golfers. Several terrified kittens had climbed up trees and refused to come down. Just when things couldn't get any worse, they did. A sudden clap of thunder was followed by a downpour. The only thing worse than a cat riot is a *wet* cat riot!

"Come on, let's get out of here," said Soldier. He was rounding up our little group and herding us out by an obscure side gate. Fortunately, he had previously scouted the place for exit routes, anticipating just such a situation. We took refuge in a nearby thickly wooded area to wait out the rain and the riot.

Epilogue

"So there you are! Where did you kitties run off to this time, the moon? Here Princess! Here Clarence! Here Whiskers! Come here and have some breakfast." We had given up trying to convince any of the humans to call Bob The Cat by his proper name. It was the morning after the Gathering Of The Cats disaster. We had stayed in the woods all night and then made our way home, catching the first bus in the morning. Mrs. Bennett opened up a couple of cans of the expensive cat food for us and also poured us a nice dish of cold milk.

That evening we were laying around on the cool grass of the back yard. The leaves on the trees twinkled like stars thanks to a stiff breeze and a full moon. The various Bennetts were sitting on the various pieces of lawn furniture on the patio, including Mary Ann who was on some sort of a break in the rocket science school year. No one had bothered to turn on the porch light, everyone content to sit in the deepening twilight. The humans conversed on typical human topics: work and school, friends and neighbors, current events and ancient history. And the weather. They love to talk about the weather. After a while the conversation lagged and one by one the family members went inside to their televisions and computers.

"This is nice," said Princess. "Just staying home, nice and peaceful."
"Yeah," I replied. "Enough adventures for a while."

THE END

CPSIA information can be obtained
at www.ICGtesting.com
Printed in the USA
BVOW03s1932140217

476190BV00001B/16/P